I0629337

A RETIRED GENTLEMAN

and other stories

Issa J Boullata

A RETIRED GENTLEMAN

and other stories

 Banipal Books
2007

First published in the UK by Banipal Books, London 2007

Copyright © 2007 Banipal Books
Original works © 2007 Issa J Boullata

The moral right of Issa J Boullata to be identified as the
author of these works has been asserted in accordance with
the Copyright, Designs and Patents Act, 1988. All rights
reserved. No part of this book may be reproduced in any
form or by any means without the prior written permission
of the publisher

A CIP record for this book is available in the British Library
ISBN 978-0-9549666-6-9

Banipal Books
P O Box 22300, LONDON W13 8ZQ, UK
www.banipal.co.uk

Set in Bembo
Printed and bound
by Lightning Source, UK&USA

For the three Barbaras I love:

my mother,

my daughter,

and my niece.

Where three persons of one name happen to be in one place at the same time, there is a hidden treasure.

An old Arab adage.

Issa J Boullata was born in Jerusalem. He is a writer, literary schol-
ar and critic, an educator and translator who started his academic
career with a PhD in Arabic literature from London University in
1969. Formerly Professor of Arabic Literature at McGill University in Montreal, he introduced and translated a ground-breaking
poetry anthology *Modern Arab Poets, 1950-1975* (1976) and has
translated a number of contemporary Arab authors including Jabra
Ibrahim Jabra, Mohamed Berrada, Emily Nasrallah and Ghada
Samman, winning translation awards for two of the works. His latest translation is the autobiography of the distinguished Palestinian
intellectual, the late Hisham Sharabi. Issa J Boullata's writings in
Arabic include a novel *A'id ila al-Quds [Returning to Jerusalem]* and
a biography *Badr Shakir al-Sayyab: His Life and Poetry*. He is a con-
tributing editor of *Banipal* magazine.

Contents

Without a court trial

"Only tell me, Sir, if you please. What is the crime I have committed against the state or the military governor, that you should arrest me and my friend?"

These were the first words he uttered after he had regained his ability to speak, following the surprise that had tied his tongue and paralysed his thinking when he saw he was being led with his friend Abdallah to the military jeep parked in front of the restaurant.

The soldier did not answer him, for he was implementing an order given him by the military governor himself a few moments before. He motioned to the jeep driver to set off.

The driver asked: "Where to?"

The soldier said curtly: "To the prison."

The military jeep drove on, in the dark of the night. The Jerusalem city streets were empty and frighteningly calm. No noise was heard except that of the running motor and the jeep's rattling as it moved.

He looked at his friend Abdallah and could hardly see his face in the dark. But he saw his eyes shining as though imploring him and saying, "Please, restrain your heroics, Hamdi. Let's see what is going to happen to us now . . ."

Hamdi, however, could not keep quiet. He repeated his earlier question to the soldier and added: "What have we done that has offended the state or the military governor?"

The soldier turned to him, training his gun in his direction, and said in a firm tone of voice: "Please keep quiet. I'm only doing my duty."

Hamdi fell silent, feeling subdued, while the military jeep drove on in the quiet streets toward the city prison. He wondered how the situation in the restaurant could have been transformed so quickly that he hardly knew what had happened.

Abdallah had decided to emigrate to the United States and had two more days before leaving the country. He had quit his job, sold his furniture, and completed all travel arrangements; he had bought an air ticket and obtained an American visa after successfully passing a medical examination. All his friends had given him private little farewell parties in their homes in the preceding few weeks, for they had not dared give him a public party under the conditions of the Jordanian military rule, during the few limited hours in the day when the curfew was lifted. As for his friends Hamdi and Jamal, they had delayed giving him a leaving party until the curfew order had been finally rescinded on that very day of that beautiful Spring of 1957. So they had invited him to a final supper in his honour at a magnificent restaurant.

The three friends arrived at the restaurant at 8.00 p.m. The maître d' led them to their reserved table and seated them with visible civility and wished them a good dinner and a happy evening.

There were only a few other diners that evening; they were all enjoying the rescinding of the curfew order as though they were birds trying their wings and flying for the first time after long detention in their cages. When the military governor entered with his commanding officers – to have dinner there – nobody paid much attention. They all seemed to be continuing to enjoy their regained freedom of movement outside their homes, or they were pretending to be indifferent, as though things had become normal again.

The military governor and his company headed for a large table that had been prepared for them, and the maître d' hovered around them. They sat and drank wine before, during and after dinner and they talked endlessly. Their presence in the restaurant sparked off furtive looks in their direction from the diners. As for the three friends, Abdallah, Hamdi and Jamal, nothing could distract them from the subject of their long-standing friendship which united them with one another. They recalled old memories, going back to their childhood, boyhood and early youth when they were growing up together in the same neighbourhood and the same school; and they hoped their good relations would continue after Abdallah's leaving for America. They drank ten bottles of beer to this friendship and dined on delicious grilled meat. After midnight, when they turned around, they noticed that all the other visitors had left except for the military governor and his commanding officers. They lowered their voices in conversation as though they suddenly felt the influence of the old terror they had experienced from childhood, with regard to everyone in power over them in their private and public lives. Their laughter froze, their jokes faded, and each of them restrained himself and could not act naturally. Each one felt he was now alone, face to face with authority in all its stark military might, despite innocent appearances. Each one felt that that authority was counting his every breath and heart beat, and listening to his every whisper.

Abdallah said in a dry voice: "Let's leave this place and hope our evening ends well."

Jamal said: "Wait for me. I'll go to the men's room first to empty some of the beer I've drunk, then I'll join you and we'll leave together."

Hamdi was feeling the pressure of the beer on his bladder too, but he preferred to stay with his friend Abdallah, as though he was afraid of leaving him alone in an ominous situation. He hoped nothing would stand in the way of his friend's leaving for America.

Then, something happened that had occurred to no

one. And things moved unexpectedly fast.

The military governor suddenly stood up and his commanding officers rose to their feet as well. He headed for the door to leave the restaurant with his company. Passing by the friends Hamdi and Abdallah sitting at the table, he gave them a dirty look they did not understand. It was as if he considered their very being there a defiance of his authority. When he reached the door, he said a few words to the soldier standing there on guard and motioned to the table of the two friends in an angry, nervous manner. He then left the restaurant with his commanding officers, got into the car waiting for him at the door, and they all drove away.

The soldier came towards the two friends and ordered them to accompany him. Meanwhile, Jamal had returned from the toilet and saw his two friends being taken to no one knew where. He was flabbergasted, and stood speechless as he watched them being led to the military jeep and driven away to what he now began to think was their detention. He knew that intervening would not save them from the unjust treatment that had been visited on many people after the recent overthrow of Jordan's cabinet, the dissolution of parliament and declaration of military rule. He saw the maître d' standing, pale and aghast, watching what was happening as though it was a nightmare. Jamal turned to him, paid the bill, and went home, his bladder saving his skin.

The policeman on duty in the prison said to the soldier:

"I can't arrest these two men or admit them to prison without a warrant or a written order from the court."

The soldier insisted: "This is the order of the military governor himself. Admit them to prison at once."

The policeman said: "I'll do it but under duress; the prison director will have to look into the matter in the morning."

In the morning, when Captain Hamza, the prison director, arrived and learned what had happened, he immediately went to the cell of those arrested. Hamdi and Abdallah had spent a sleepless night, they had been continually getting up to go to a tin container in the corner and empty the beer in their bladders. The other two men in the cell with them laughed at the ironical situation when told the story, for, unlike the new inmates, they had both been accused of secretly belonging to an Arab socialist political party banned by the government and had spent more than thirty days in prison already without a court trial.

Captain Hamza looked at Hamdi and Abdallah through the iron bars of the door with some unexpected sympathy. Then he said to the guard: "Unlock the door."

The four prisoners were astonished. Hamdi and Abdallah stood up while the other two remained lying on the thin pad on the floor which served as a mattress; it was as though they were not impressed and were seeing an ordinary, daily scene.

Captain Hamza said: "Come on. Get out, all of you.

You're free. What are you waiting for?"

The two men lying down got up, astounded.

The prison director added: "What's the matter with you? Do you like staying in prison? I said 'Get out!' It's all over. A coup d'état took place in the small hours of last night, and this morning the new cabinet ordered that all those arrested should be released."

The prisoners looked at one another in disbelief.

Captain Hamza added: "As for the military governor and his company, the new authorities have arrested them and sent them far away to a desert prison . . . without a court trial!"

Bar-room confessions

I am not fond of drinking, although once in a while I do take a drink or two with a friend when an occasion calls for it. My friend Sam, on the other hand, is the exact opposite. He likes to drink every evening but can refrain when occasion calls for restraint. However, he always prefers to drink with a friend, he hates to drink alone. I am therefore not the ideal boon companion for him despite our strong friendship, which goes back to our school days in Lebanon. When he invited me to join him for a drink at a local bar in Montreal, I was surprised. He said that the drinks would be on him.

Having recently arrived in Montreal from Beirut with his wife Mayy while the uncivil war was raging, he was still looking for a job and his money was understandably running out. His wife had found a good position at the Bank of Montreal and was beginning to feel at home in the city. By contrast, Sam was still unsettled and disoriented. He and Mayy had no children but they were planning on having at least a couple, as he once told me in Beirut.

Sam and I sat at a table beside the window. The street outside was crowded with people as the evening fell on the city. Some customers were dropping in to take advantage of the reduced prices during what is called the "Happy Hour", between 5 and 6 pm. Sam ordered his usual drink of cognac and for me a glass of red wine.

"There is nothing like Cabernet Sauvignon," I said.

"Cognac is quicker," he remarked.

"It depends on why one drinks," I suggested. "I never drink to get drunk."

"I never do, either," he replied. "I drink to while away time, heavy time. It seems to me the hours are long and burdensome and empty until I begin drinking with a friend. All my other friends had reasons not to join me this evening and so I am happy that you are here with me now."

"It's my pleasure, Sam," I said. "But, tell me, how is your search for a job going?"

"Oh, it's going all right, I suppose. I got employers' names and addresses from the Canadian Human Resources Centre, and I applied for a few jobs and have been interviewed for some. I'm still waiting but I expect that in a few weeks I'll be employed."

The waiter brought our drinks and a bowl of salted peanuts to share between us.

"To your health," Sam raised his glass and eagerly took

a long sip of cognac.

"A la vôtre, my friend," I said and put the glass to my lips.

"And is Mayy enjoying her job at the bank?"

"She is," he said. "Mayy's a happy-go-lucky person and can easily adjust to new conditions. I can't . . . I don't know whether I'll ever get accustomed to this Canadian weather with its severe winters or to the fast pace of life in Montreal all year round."

"I felt the same way when I first arrived here a couple of years ago. But one gets used to it gradually, you know."

"What gets me is that my home life is affected by this change. In Beirut, I knew my place, Mayy knew hers, and we lived a nice life together. Here, I don't know. She holds the purse strings, she does the shopping, she runs the home, she decides how and where we are to spend our evenings . . . I love her dearly and don't dare displease her, let alone contradict her."

Sam took another long sip of his cognac, almost emptying his glass. I sensed the tension in his voice and knew he was letting me in on his private life. He often did that in Beirut too and his conversations used to become more and more intimate with each successive drink. I thought perhaps he now needed to let off steam a little: he was without work, his wife had become the bread-winner in Canada before he had been able to, and so he might have some feelings of jealousy or inadequacy. I thought that perhaps that was why he invited me for a drink, knowing

I have always been a good and sympathetic listener.

"The other day," he began, "she bought a pair of pink chiffon stockings, those new-fashioned ones with darker transparent floral designs. I said to her: 'Mayy, you have enough stockings, my dear. Why do you have to buy more?' She said: 'Oh, but these are the new fashion, Sam.' I said: 'Yes, I know. But can we afford to keep up with new fashions, my dear, now that we are immigrant refugees in this country?' She said: 'Don't you want me to be like all the other young women here?' I replied: 'Of course, I do. But such inessential things can wait until I have a job at least. Can't they?' She said: 'I have a job, Sam. Can't I spend my money on what I like?' And she began crying. 'Come, come,' I said. 'Spend it as you like, my love, and I'll give you more to spend when I have a job.' I hugged her, dried her tears and kissed her."

Sam drank the rest of his cognac in one gulp and ordered another glass.

"You're hardly touching your wine," he noted. "Drink up and let me order another glass for you.

"No, Sam. You know I don't drink much. You go ahead, drink as you wish and let me sip my wine slowly and enjoy your company."

He said: "Sorry to bother you with my stories. You're not married, but I know you understand my situation better than my married friends. I hope I'm not boring you?"

"Of course not, Sam. You can tell me whatever you

want and I'll listen and respond. I think Mayy is a lovely woman and you are fortunate to have such a wife. Your happiness with her was the talk of the town in Beirut. And I have no doubt it will continue to be so here in Montreal or anywhere. Only one needs patience in such circumstances, and everything will be fine."

"I have all the patience in the world," he said, "and I hope it works."

This gave me the first inkling that it was not working, or that something was wrong. Sam was fidgety, looking around him and at his watch and drinking big gulps of his cognac. At times our conversation was interrupted by long periods of silence until I started the ball rolling again. He ordered a third, then a fourth glass of cognac while I was still drinking my first glass of wine. I wondered whether he really was in trouble or simply undergoing one of those periods in one's life when everything seems to have gone wrong, when life seems to have become meaningless, when living seems to be a waste of one's efforts and a time to regret lost opportunities, when one needs to reorient one's life and may be liable to make mistakes or even commit fatal blunders. I knew that if this was the case, Sam would be in great need of sincere friends to stand by him and help.

He turned to me at one point and said apropos of no relevant previous thought: "You know how much I would like to have a child. We once spoke about that and I told you I would like to have at least a couple."

"Yes," I said, agreeing.

"What would you say if I told you I almost had one?"

"What do you mean?"

"Well, you see, Mayy became pregnant but did not tell me. Then she decided to have an abortion and also did not tell me. When she could not find a gynaecologist to agree, she resorted to a quack who gave her a drug which she took at home to bring on the abortion she wanted. Then she became sick and was forced to tell me. She had to stay in bed for several days and I remained at her bedside and nursed her.

"When she recovered, we had a talk about what had happened. I said: 'My dear Mayy, how in the world could you embark on an act as important as this without telling me?' She said: 'I did not want to bother you. Besides, my body is mine, nobody else's.' I said: 'No, my dear. When a couple get married, they become one body. As husband and wife we cleave to each other till death do us part.' She did not agree and said to me: 'Oh, Sam. Those are old ideas. They don't work in the New World. Don't you read the Canadian and American newspapers and magazines? Abortion is a woman's choice, nobody else's.' A woman's choice, she says, a woman's choice! What do you think of that, my friend?"

I did not know what to say but I knew something was wrong between Sam and Mayy.

He then continued: "And that was not the end of it. She kept accusing me of not being sensitive to what she had gone through. 'I need to keep my job,' she said. 'I will lose it in the end if I become pregnant and have the baby. It was for your sake I decided on abortion as a solution. Do you understand? I would love to have a baby, Sam. How do you think I felt when I went to the toilet and let the blood gush out of me? I saw pieces of my baby being flushed down the toilet . . . I still dream of it . . . I see it now, even as I talk to you . . . I'll see it all my life . . . It's etched into my memory . . . It's on my conscience . . . Do you understand?' And she started crying and sobbing wildly. I hugged her tenderly and kissed her. 'No, no, my love,' I said, comforting her and caressing her cheeks and wiping away her tears. 'There are laws protecting the jobs of pregnant women,' I added, 'and there are ways to prevent pregnancy. All I say is that we should have discussed the matter and come to an agreement together. Why should you bear the responsibility for this alone? Abortion is a huge step to take and we should have decided together what had to be done.' 'What's done is done,' she said as though to put an end to the conversation . . . And she began to drift away from me, day after day. In the end, I could not reach her any more. Our love was dying and making love has been a constant confrontation."

Sam ordered his fifth glass of cognac.

All of a sudden, he stood up. He smiled and looked towards the door of the bar as a gorgeous woman entered. She was a tall woman with blue eyes and wore a white silk blouse with ruffled sleeves, black skin-tight pants, and high heels. She seemed to be in her forties and looked as though she had seen it all. She walked towards us with a sure step, smiling engagingly.

Sam held out his hand to her. "You're right on time," he said as he shook her hand. "Let me introduce you to my friend Fadil Karam from the good old days in Lebanon. Fadil, this is my friend Mireille Archambault who owns a business in town. Please sit down."

As the waiter brought Sam's fifth glass of cognac, Sam asked: "What would you like to drink, Mireille?"

"Perrier, please. Thank you."

Sam explained: "Mireille runs a menswear boutique on Sherbrooke Street and is in need of a salesman."

"Oh! Nice meeting you, Ma'am," I mumbled.

Pretty soon we were all engaged in conversation on a variety of topics. But increasingly I noticed Sam's searching appraisal of Mireille and was aware of her basking in the warmth of his eyes. There was no doubt she was intelligent, worldly, and powerful; her beauty crowned her other qualities but did not submerge them – in fact it enhanced them. She was well-read and fully bilingual – her English was as good as her native French when we exchanged ideas in either language as many Montreal people often do. It was evident that Sam and Mireille were enjoying each other's company. I was the odd man out in the end, and I excused myself at about 10 pm, way past the "Happy Hour", after having finally finished my second glass of red wine.

I did not see Sam until a week later. He told me he had landed a well-paid job at Mireille Archambault's boutique. I congratulated him and offered him my best wishes. He looked hesitant for a moment, but then thanked me and said: "But, Fadil, I should tell you this: Mayy is filing for divorce."

"What?" I exclaimed.

"She says I neglect her and verbally abuse her. She claims I am stingy and insensitive to her needs. She says I curtail her freedom and choke the development of her personality. She believes I don't love her any longer, and she wants out."

"Sam," I entreated. "Is there no way for reconciliation? I'll do my best to bring you together."

"No, Fadil," he said in surrender. "She's made up her mind as firmly as when she decided on that abortion. It's a woman's choice, she insists. What's done is done!"

"That's sheer stupidity, if you'll excuse me."

"No, Fadil," Sam said. "It's the Lebanese uncivil war finally getting to our private life. If there had been no war and we had stayed in Lebanon, we would not have had this unfortunate conclusion to our married life. I did my best but I failed. What's done is done. Mayy is right, after all."

Third in Command

George Sa'di would never have dreamt that within a year of his arrival in Canada as a landed immigrant, he would become an executive officer of one of the most aggressive small investment and trading firms in the country. He had graduated with a Master's degree in business administration from the University of Haifa in Israel, but very few people knew the price in hard work he had had to pay as an Arab Israeli to achieve that. Having left his limited opportunities of employment back at home, he was today third in command at Sleeman & Son in Vancouver.

He remembered how insecure and frightened he was on first arriving in this vast country, knowing virtually no one the first few days after his arrival. But thanks to a message he had had to deliver to a Mr Rasheed Sleeman from an old lady in Nazareth, Israel, he was now enjoying a coveted and secure position in which he could use his university training as well as his personal potential to the full, allowing him to put behind him all the sweat and labour of his early youth, when he often worked carrying bricks, stones, and mortar on construction sites. Canada was indeed a land of opportunity for all those seeking progress who were ready to work hard – but he could not discount the element of good luck in his present situation.

He still remembered the day he first met Mr Sleeman who, until then, was a mere name to him. He had been told Mr Sleeman was the owner and manager of a firm he had established in Canada several years earlier. But George Sa'di had no idea he would become involved in this firm, and in a way he had never anticipated.

On that day, when he first met Mr Sleeman, he went to the address he had found in the telephone directory. It turned out to be one of the high-rise buildings in down-town Vancouver. He had not made an appointment but boldly walked in, saying he had a personal message from Nazareth for Mr Sleeman, and the secretary showed him into the office of her boss who, contrary to his custom, agreed to see him without prior appointment.

"Good morning, Mr Sleeman," George Sa'di said respectfully, now cowed by the plush office he found himself in, on the twenty-fifth floor of the high-rise building. "I'm grateful you've allowed me to see you without an appointment, sir. Knowing how valuable your time is, I'll come to the point immediately . . ."

The telephone bell rang and George hesitated. Mr Sleeman motioned him to a leather armchair, then picked up the receiver and listened. Then he said: "Yes, please. Sell the whole oil shipment at once. One million dollars is a sufficient profit by today's prices. Sell and call me again after that. Thanks."

Putting down the telephone receiver, Mr Sleeman turned to George: "Sorry for the interruption. Yes, you were saying . . .?"

"Oh, Mr Sleeman. I was beginning to say . . . I'm a new immigrant in Canada. I arrived in Vancouver only a couple of days ago from Nazareth, Israel. Before leaving, I promised your aunt Olga that I'd see you as soon as I could, and that I'd tell you about your sister Stephanie . . ."

Mr Sleeman interrupted: "What aunt Olga and what sister Stephanie are you talking about? What did you say your name was . . .?"

"Sa'di. George Sa'di, sir."

"Well, Mr Sa'di. I have no aunt Olga and no sister Stephanie."

"Yes, you do, Mr Sleeman. And that's why I'm here to let you know . . ."

"Please, go on."

"I was told it's a long story that goes back to 1948 in Palestine. It's a story that is more than fifty years old now. You must have been six years old then, and you may remember very little of it, if anything at all."

Mr Sleeman began to show some interest. He knew that when he was six, his family lived in Jaffa, Palestine. He still remembered that his father had to run away with him one day in May of 1948 when their home was destroyed by a terrible explosion during the fighting between the Zionists and the Palestinians in the last days of the British Mandate. He was told that his mother and sister had died at home under the rubble and that he and his father had been spared because they happened to be both out, buying food. When his father later dared to return home furtively to check, despite the ongoing sniping and bombing, and saw his home in a hopeless heap of stones and smouldering debris, he decided in utter despair to take his son Rasheed and flee the city.

"I'm told," George continued, "that your sister Stephanie was saved from the rubble of your home in Jaffa, six days after it was destroyed by an explosion. The Israelis had occupied Jaffa and were beginning to comb the town and make it secure for their forces. As you may know, the majority of the Palestinian inhabitants of Jaffa had fled, mostly taking to the Mediterranean in boats bound for Beirut and Gaza; but some escaped on foot inland into Palestine, eventually reaching the hills of Ramallah, north of Jerusalem. As the Israeli fighters reached the site of your home in Jaffa, they heard a child's faint cry coming from underneath the rubble. So their experts began to dig and finally found your three-year-old sister."

"What about her mother?" Mr Sleeman asked, beginning to think there might be some truth in what George was relating.

"I'm sorry, Mr Sleeman. I was told your mother had

died and that her arched body under a steel beam had saved Stephanie. The child was rushed to a hospital in Tel Aviv. She was dehydrated and needed immediate medical care. She stayed in hospital for a month, then she was released to social workers in the Israeli Department of Social Welfare."

George paused. Mr Sleeman looked at him intently, then asked: "And what happened to Stephanie?"

"Well, sir, I'm told it took the social welfare workers about two years to locate your aunt Olga in Nazareth, and she kindly agreed to take care of your sister. She is not really your aunt but rather a distant relative of your father. She was the nearest relative they could find in Israel after long investigation, all other relatives having died or fled to safe refuge elsewhere. She is about eighty years old now. But I promised her I'd tell you . . ."

"And Stephanie would now be in her mid-fifties," Mr Sleeman suggested.

"Yes, sir. And she lives in Amman with her husband and three children."

Mr. Sleeman became pensive. "What a small world!" he thought to himself. "And what a miserable life the Palestinians lead in their diaspora and in their homeland!"

He remembered how, as a child of six, he had had to walk and walk with his father for hours on end, away from Jaffa, avoiding the main roads and taking the rough and rocky paths in the countryside, stopping only for brief rests, then joining other groups of Palestinian refugees from various coastal towns and villages – men, women, and children trekking eastward with the belongings that they could carry. They reached the hills of Ramallah the next day and local inhabitants gave them food and shelter until the International Red Cross, the Red Crescent and, later, the UNRWA offered them help in an organized way.

The telephone bell rang again. Mr Sleeman picked up the receiver and listened. Then he said: "Sell all my Nortel holdings. Do you hear me, ALL my Nortel shares." He listened for a moment then said: "I don't care what Canadian Finance Minister Mr Paul Martin says. He has his government finances and the Canadian economy to take care of, and I have my business. Nortel shares have reached their highest price and, actually, they are now overvalued. They are bound to have a big fall soon. Please, sell high, now." Then he added after a pause: "With the proceeds, you now have the cash flow to buy one million barrels of oil from the United Arab Emirates for Turkey, to honour the agreement I signed yesterday with the Turkish Minister of Energy for the delivery of six oil shipments over the next six months."

Turning to George and continuing the conversation as though there had been no interruption, he asked: "And how did the lady you call my aunt Olga know I am here?"

"Oh, only by coincidence, sir. A graduate of the University of British Columbia returned home recently to Nazareth from Vancouver and spoke highly of you. And when she heard your name, she immediately knew you must be Stephanie's brother."

"You see, Mr Sa'di," Mr. Sleeman began: "I don't know this lady. However, I do remember my sister Stephanie but I have long given her up for dead. I grew up in Ramallah and was educated at the Friends Boys' School. My father took good care of me. When the rump Palestinian territory, called 'the West Bank', was annexed and ruled by Jordan, he worked as a policeman in Jordan's police force until he died twelve years ago, God bless his soul. After graduating from school, I went to the United Arab Emirates to work. That's where I got married and divorced, made a fortune, and established good business contacts that are of great help to me now."

There was a knock at the door and a handsome, smartly-dressed young man in his mid-twenties entered.

"This is my son, Kamal," said Mr. Sleeman. "Kamal, this is Mr George Sa'di who has recently arrived from the old country."

Shaking hands with George, Kamal said cheerfully: "Oh, you're from Palestine? Glad to meet you, George."

"Er . . . From Israel . . . from Nazareth. Glad to meet you too."

George, who was about the same age as Kamal, liked the young man's spontaneity but felt he was inexperienced and rather naive.

After receiving ten $100 bills from his father, Kamal excused himself and left the office. Mr Sleeman turned to

George and asked: "Have you found a job, Mr Sa'di?"

"No, not yet, sir," he said and proceeded to give an oral resumé of his business qualifications without being asked.

Mr. Sleeman listened, nodding in apparent appreciation, then he said: "Would you like to work for me?"

"Yes, indeed, Mr. Sleeman," George answered with visible enthusiasm. "I would do any job you would want me to."

"Fine. I'll pay you $4,000 a month. You'll work from 9 to 5, five days a week except for official holidays, and you'll have a paid two-week leave per year and the usual Canadian social benefits."

George Sa'di was elated and could not believe his ears.

"Thank you, sir," he said. "And what are my duties?"

"Well, you'll begin tomorrow and I'll have you do office work so that you can learn the ropes. You will also do an additional specific duty for the next four months. You may find you'll have to work after hours or at the weekend at times, but you're not obliged to and it's up to you. After this period, I'll give you other duties and I'll consider you for a raise, depending on results."

"But what's the additional specific duty besides office work that you want me to do in the next four months, Mr Sleeman?"

"Train my son, Kamal. Teach him to be like you: forthcoming, outgoing, imaginative, ready to take the initiative, to be of service to others. Teach him to be wise in the ways of this world. You see, he's about your age. But he dropped out of university before completing his first year. I've employed him in my office but he has learned nothing. I've recently made him a partner in my firm but all he does is claim a thousand dollars per week, on account. I want him to be responsible, responsive, but none of my clerks could help him. I suppose it is my fault in the first place. After my divorce, I took custody of him as a boy of six but I think I was too busy making my fortune in the United Arab Emirates during his formative years. I hope it's not too late now. When I pressed him lately to come up with a business project to work on, he suggested buying a Ferrari and participating in the Formula One car race at the Montreal Grand Prix next May. Totally unrealistic and unacceptable. He is crazy about fast cars. He has a Jaguar and spurns my Rolls Royce. I think I am a good judge of character, Mr Sa'di, and I believe you can help. What I want you to do is to make him see the real world. That's your additional specific duty, George. May I call you George?"

"Yes, indeed, Mr Sleeman. And I'll do my best."

In the following four months, George Sa'di managed to become a bosom friend of Kamal. From books, magazines, and newspapers, he learned all about racing cars and speedways and racing series in order to win over the young man's attention in conversation. He even accompanied him to car races and winners' parties. Gently and calculatingly, he helped him measure the physical and financial risks of car racing against other means of enjoying life's excitements. He finally got him to quit his obsession with cars and appreciate the exciting work in the investment market. Together, they built up a successful investment project and a promising portfolio with which Mr Sleeman was extremely pleased.

One day, Kamal said to George as they sat down over a cup of coffee: "You've changed my life, George, and you're now my best friend. But there's something I'd like to say to you in full confidence, may I? Perhaps you can help me."

"Of course, my friend."

"You know how much I love and respect my father. But I'd like to tell you that, in the last five years, he has stolen almost every single girlfriend I had. I'm not the playboy he thinks I am and believes he should protect. I do love my girlfriends even if I have no intention of getting married yet. I'm still young and I like to have fun with them. It's exciting and exhilarating. I turned to the thrill of racing cars only after my father's continual intervention in my relationships with my girlfriends. I can't compete with him, especially given his power to attract them with lavish gifts and his social status in high-class circles. It's rather he who is the playboy – and an experienced, rich one at that. Can you help me keep his hands off my present girlfriends?"

George felt he was in a dilemma and had never thought he would ever be asked to intervene in matters of the heart. But he said he would think about it.

He did not sleep well that night, thinking.

On the following day, Mr Sleeman called George to his office and informed him that he had finally established communications with his sister and her family in Amman, and had sent them air tickets to come to Canada for a visit. He then thanked him profusely for what he had done for Kamal over the four months. He also expressed his appreciation of George's proficiency in office work and his growing expertise in handling investments, and said he was giving him a raise of $2,000 a month and greater responsibility for the technology sector of the business.

George thought for a moment then said: "I'm sorry to disappoint you, Mr. Sleeman, but I was planning to come and see you today in order to submit my resignation."

"What . . . ! Aren't you happy with us?"

"I am, Mr Sleeman. But there's a personal problem I can't solve if I stay with Sleeman & Son."

"Well, maybe I can help you solve it, if you permit me."

"Yes, you can, Mr Sleeman. But it's rather difficult."

"Let me try, at least. For I need you and I want you to stay with us."

Politely but firmly, George put the matter squarely before Mr Sleeman with regard to Kamal's girlfriends and he ended by saying: "Kamal is a good person, Mr Sleeman. I'm sure you don't want to lose him; for I think you will, and perhaps tragically, if things continue as they have been."

Mr Sleeman felt he was being chastened but he knew he had asked for it. He was silent for a while, somewhat embarrassed. He did not deny anything, he did not defend himself, he did not offer any justification. He felt he only wanted the good of his son and to keep this daring and helpful new employee of his.

"Yes, indeed. Kamal is a good person," he said at long last. "And so are you, George. You're helping me to see things clearly and to keep communications with my son open. I've had my fill in life, I suppose, and it's his turn now. I will leave him and his girlfriends alone. I want him to be happy and I want Sleeman & Son to continue to be successful too. Will you stay with us?"

"I will, sir, as long as I can be of service," George said in relief.

And that is how he eventually came to be third in command at Sleeman & Son.

Harvest of the Years

When I saw Jimmy Ferris last week in Hartford, Connecticut, I was shocked at how he looked. I had not seen him for the last ten years. I had been transferred by my company from Hartford to Washington, DC to manage the head office there. He had stayed in Hartford to take care of his growing private business. We had spoken with each other on the phone a number of times since I left, and for a while we exchanged Christmas cards. But then we gradually lost touch, what with our increasing family commitments, job preoccupations, new friends and interests, and – yes – laziness!

Jimmy and I were friends, not only when we both lived and worked in Hartford, but long before that. As a matter of fact, he was my superior for several years when I was a young government employee at the Department of Statistics in Amman, Jordan. Jimmy Ferris was then known by his original Arabic name, Jamil Faris, and all twelve employees in his charge in the Bureau of Population Statistics at the Department liked him. He was considerate but firm and knew how to get the best out of all his subordinates. Although he was a dozen years older than me and was married with two children, a son and a daughter of high school age, he created a special friendly bond with me. I had recently graduated from college at the time and was not yet married. I appreciated his warm feelings toward me and his encouraging advice that I should go to the United States for graduate studies in economics. He felt that with a higher degree I would do much better in life than being a government employee in statistics, and that I had the brains and the ability to rise to high positions.

Eventually I left Amman for the United States as an immigrant, studied economics at Boston University where I earned a Master's degree, and then landed a promising corporate job in Hartford. Likewise, Jamil Faris emigrated to the United States with his family and came to live in Hartford, where he started a little fast-food business and where his grown children went to Trinity College. We resumed our friendly relations when we discovered we both lived in the same city and came to know other newly-arrived Arab immigrants in the area and many Arab-Americans established there for two or three generations. When he became an American citizen, he changed his name to James Ferris but all his friends called him Jimmy.

"Jimmy", I said one day. "How's your fast-food business

doing?"

"Come and see for yourself," he said.

I took him at his word and dropped by his place one evening. It was a small shop with five sets of tables and chairs, and a counter with a glass front in which colourful bowls of salad and sandwich ingredients were neatly displayed. He and his wife Sandra were behind the counter and they both welcomed me heartily. When I declined their offer of a sandwich, he gave me a cup of coffee and sat with me at a table.

Customers kept coming in and going out, and Sandra served them promptly. Most of them walked out with their sandwiches into the busy mall outside; very few lingered or sat at the tables in the shop.

"You seem to have a brisk business here," I commented.

"Yes," Jimmy said, "especially at this hour before the movies start. When the movies end and the theaters at the mall let out crowds of movie-goers, we are overwhelmed by customers. In fact, I'm thinking of hiring help."

"Congratulations," I said. "You must like this job better than your former responsibilities as a boss at a bureau of statistics."

"Yes, I do. I'm working for myself now, not for the government as before. Sandra and I are thinking of opening another shop in the new West Hartford mall and possibly others elsewhere later on."

"That's good news. And how are your children doing?" I asked.

"They're both fine. Sam will graduate with a Bachelor of Science degree in June and plans to go to the University of Chicago next year to study computer science and get a graduate degree. Kate is a sophomore in arts and has two more years to go. But, you know, we hardly see them. Sandra and I are busy at the shop from seven in the morning till midnight. We're both tired by the time we go home and in the morning we leave before the children are up."

"Well, that's life in America," I said in sympathy.

"Yes, but it is not the high quality I expected. The pace of life here is so much faster than in the old country, and it is superficial and materialistic. We're grateful we found an Orthodox church in nearby Wethersfield to belong to, like we did in Amman. On Sunday mornings, our children go there to worship but only one parent can go with them, because the other has to attend to the shop. So Sandra and I alternate every week, and thus we hope to keep up our religious tradition at least."

I sensed some wistful tone in Jimmy's speech.

"There's a price for everything in life," I said. "Yours is not bad at all."

"You're right," he responded. "What matters for Sandra and me is to give our children the best education and to prepare them for a better life than ours. You know, I only have a high school education and Sandra likewise. It has been by dint of my wide reading that after high school in Jordan I increased my general knowledge and achieved a good and rising position in the government's employ. I was lucky, I suppose. But my luckiest thing was marrying Sandra, a wonderful woman – as you know."

"Yes, yes," I said as I looked at her behind the counter, where she was busy making sandwiches and cheerfully serving each customer.

I looked back at Jimmy and Sandra as I was leaving the shop and they were waving to me, and I noticed the big sign over the door that said JIMMY'S PLACE in neon lights.

After a two-year absence in Detroit, I returned to Hartford to resume my work in the company at a higher rank. I was married to Selma, a lovely young woman of Arab origin I had met in Detroit, and we had a beautiful baby girl we named Susan. At Bradley International Airport, where we landed on our return to Hartford from Detroit, I saw a shop with a JIMMY'S PLACE neon sign. But Jimmy was not there, and somebody else was running it. I told Selma about my friend Jimmy and his family.

Shortly afterwards, I called Jimmy and then one afternoon went to see him at the shop in Hartford. He and Sandra welcomed me cordially and they both came to sit with me at a table over a cup of coffee. They were interested to learn all about my new family and my recent promotion at the company. Three employees were behind the counter serving customers and their sandwich menu was now richer and included Arab varieties such as falafel, hummous, and chicken and lamb gyro.

"I see you've improved your menu," I observed.

"Indeed," said Jimmy proudly. "Moreover, we now have twenty-one fast-food shops in several Connecticut localities."

"We're planning to open two more in Massachusetts," added Sandra with a glint of exultation.

"You're not going to put Howard Johnson out of business now, are you?" I teased.

"Of course not," said Jimmy quickly. "We're offering people healthy food," he added in a light-hearted, commercial plug-in. "Let the customers choose. They're always right."

"We might start a Jimmy's Hotel," ventured Sandra earnestly.

"No, no," said Jimmy. "That's way beyond our immediate plans."

"You never know . . ." I said. "With a wife like Sandra, many things are possible!"

"Thank God for Sandra," he said. "But our plans are to manage the shops we have in the best manner and to maintain the high quality of our only restaurant, JIMMY'S RESTAURANT, on Main Street in Hartford."

"Oh, you have a restaurant too?"

"Yes. It is the jewel of my business. And I am inviting you and Selma to dinner at my restaurant so that you may see it, and Sandra and I may enjoy your company. You see, I believe eating should be a civilized exercise. Fast food eaten on the run, using paper napkins and styrofoam cups and plates, is not my idea of civilised eating. Even if you sit down to eat your fast food with a flimsy plastic fork and knife at a bare table provided with all sorts of condiments, it is not civilised eating. There is a world of difference between that and a restaurant like mine, where you have comfortable chairs and tables covered with white tablecloths; where you have linen napkins, porcelain dishes and plates, real silverware, and crystal glasses; where you are met by a properly attired maître d' and served by properly attired, polite, and deft waiters; and where you have a printed, rich menu and a good wine list, suggesting a well-trained chef in the kitchen and a well-kept wine cellar. The ambience is quiet, with perhaps light music and soft lights in the evenings. That's civilised eating, sir, that's civilised eating."

"Indeed it is," I concurred.

I looked at Sandra's face. Her bright eyes smiled to me as I pondered what her husband was saying. Her soft skin showed early signs of wrinkling but her face, framed by her greying hair, had a lofty expression of dignity. I looked at Jimmy and noted his firm eyes that bespoke a strong will. His receding hairline and wrinkled face told of his long life of hard work.

When Selma and I dined with Jimmy and Sandra at JIMMY'S RESTAURANT a week later, we had a memorable evening together. The restaurant was almost full and the people there were the elite of the Greater Hartford area. Our sumptuous dinner was enlivened by intelligent and friendly conversation. But as we drank our after-dinner drinks, I heard Jimmy make a remark that made me think he was not yet happy in his life. There seemed to be something he wanted to achieve that was not yet quite clear to his inner vision of himself and his world.

"You must come and visit us in our new home," he began. "It's a lovely, quiet place in Farmington half an hour's drive from Hartford. Our friends like it, and Sandra and I think it is a nice home to spend the rest of our lives in. We've both worked very hard and deserve some rest eventually, don't you think so? We spent our youth, our whole life, working, planning, expanding our business, providing for Sam and Kate, educating them, creating for them the good life we want them to have, denying ourselves many things in order to achieve these ends. Now we can't go back to live our life as we want. It's gone. But our children are our treasure. They live a free life in this country. Each of them has a car. They have all their needs and a promising future ahead. I will be the happiest man to see Sam in two years with a PhD and Kate with a Master's, and both eventually established in their professions, married happily with lovely children, our grandchildren, visiting us at our Farmington home and staying over on weekends and holidays. Our home is big enough for that. Do come and visit us."

"Thanks. We will, Jimmy," I said. "You certainly have beautiful dreams for the future, and you and Sandra deserve all good things."

But we never had the opportunity of visiting Jimmy and
Sandra in their Farmington home, for I was soon transferred by my company from Hartford to Washington as
manager of the head office there and I gradually lost
touch with Jimmy in the ensuing ten years.

When I returned to Hartford last week on a company
mission, I thought I should try to see Jimmy and Sandra,
if only for good old times' sake. I had some difficulty
locating Jimmy but I was told he would most likely be at
his office at JIMMY'S RESTAURANT.

Indeed, he was. But I had the shock of my life to see
him.

Jimmy was haggard. He must have lost half his weight.
His eyes were sunken and dim. His head was totally bald
and his back was bent. When he stood up and came over
from his desk to meet me, he faltered and his skinny hand
trembled as he stretched his arm to greet me.

I shook his weak hand and missed his earlier, strong
grip. His voice was husky when he expressed his surpise
at seeing me but it was warm and cordial.

"Sit down, sit down," he said. "You remind me of my
youth. How are you, my friend? How is Selma? How is
Susan? She must be a teenager now . . ."

After I informed him about my family, I asked, "And
how are you, Jimmy, and how is Sandra?"

"Sandra is at home. She's fine. Kate is with her, she has
come from Boston to visit us with her daughter, Reema,

and her son Ramsay. Her husband, Karim, is a nice young Palestinian she met at university. He has a good position at an engineering firm in Boston."

"And how is Sam? Did he get his PhD?"

Jimmy did not answer. He looked at the palms of his empty, trembling hands. He then looked up at me and attempted to speak. His lips quivered, his chin twitched. Then he broke into a sob and burst into tears.

I stood up and went to him. I put my arm around him as he sat on his chair at the desk. I felt his whole body shaking.

"It's okay. Take it easy, Jimmy," I said trying to comfort him.

When he regained his composure, he wiped his tears with the back of his hands. He looked bravely at me and said, "Sam died."

I did not know what to say.

"He was driving back home from Chicago for the Christmas holiday in his final PhD year," he explained. "There was a blizzard and visibility on the highway was almost nil. A young woman flagged down his car. She had a flat tyre and was desperate for help. He pulled over and put her spare tyre on. As he was returning to his car to resume his trip home, an eighteen-wheeler hit him and he died instantly."

"Oh, Jimmy . . . I'm really sorry."

"My son, my treasure!" he said. "This is the harvest of my years."

A moment later he added, "However, seeing and hearing and touching Reema and Ramsay, and being with them and talking to them gives me some relief."

He looked pensively at me, then suddenly regained a sense of urgency as though he had remembered something.

"Oh, I've forgotten my manners," he said. "I haven't offered you a cup of coffee or anything else."

"Thank you," I said. "I had a cup of coffee just before I came here."

"Well then. I have a better idea. If you're willing, I'll drive you to Farmington; you'll see Sandra and Kate and my lovely grandchildren. They'll all be thrilled to see you."

"Fine," I said as I marvelled at Jimmy's change of mood. "This is an opportunity I cannot miss."

As we drove up Farmington Avenue, Jimmy talked and I mostly listened. I was amazed at how philosophical he had become. Mature in years and having gone through periods of hard work and painful experience, he now had a deep feeling of how valuable every single moment of life was. He gave me the impression that nothing counted in life but love and happiness. And every moment, however fleeting, that offered love and happiness had to be seized and enjoyed to the full.

Mentioning his son Sam in passing, he said, "I had him for twenty-five years to enjoy. Can you imagine that? Twenty-five years! The moment of his birth gave me an incomparable feeling of elation that strengthened my will to live. And from that moment on, every single new experience of his was mine, renewing my life and drawing me to enjoy its eagerness, its expectations, its wonders, its surprises. He was not meant to live longer and that definitely saddened me. But that made me also realise how much more I should enjoy the remaining days of my life with those I love, both family and friends, and how much more I should try to make them happy."

I immediately understood why he invited me to go home with him to see his loved ones. I was glad I accepted his invitation and I looked forward to being there with him and them.

All is Vanity

Gaby and Randa were high school sweethearts in Alexandria, Egypt, but after graduation they went their separate ways because their families had plans that did not take theirs into consideration.

"Nonsense," Randa's mother had said. "High school infatuations lead to nothing, or else to disaster. We're leaving soon for Canada as immigrants and you'll come with us. You'll go to the University of Toronto, and I'm sure you'll find a young man after your heart there."

And Randa did: he was the same young man, the same Gaby she had loved for two years in high school back in Alexandria, for his family had come to Canada as immigrants too. He was studying to become a chemical engineer, while she was majoring in English literature, at the same University of Toronto.

They graduated together in the same year and their parents were proud to announce their engagement, even before Gaby began working for Dupont Canada Inc.

Randa decided to go on with her education and earn a Master's degree and then teach in high school. But she dropped out when, a couple of months after the wedding and despite precautions, she discovered she was going to have a baby.

They named the baby Mark Antony after his two grandfathers, not intending any allusions to Roman history or Shakespearean drama. He grew up to be a nice chubby boy and when he began to go to school, Randa was able at last to proceed with her higher education to become a teacher. She entered the Master's programme again and put behind her the years of baby care, night feeding, diaper washing, tending to illnesses, and confinement to the house. She was determined not to have any more children and was bent on completing her studies, earning an MA, and building up her own career.

Gaby was by now a responsible manager at Dupont Canada Inc. and was looking forward to moving to higher ranks in the company. He enjoyed his evenings at home with Mark Antony as they played together and studied together. He read him a story at bedtime, put him to bed, then watched a television programme or two before going to bed himself. Randa would be alone in the study, reading or preparing her next day's assignments, that is, if she was not late coming home from a night lecture, a drama presentation, or a social function at the university.

Gaby thought that the couple of years before Randa

finished her studies would pass quickly, and that they were worth enduring. For, truth be told, he was beginning to feel lonely and his social life was becoming too limited. He gave Mark Antony much love and the boy took it, but could not give back all the love that Gaby needed, even when the boy grew older and became a tough young guy of thirteen, as by then his interests were radiating away from home, not towards it. Randa understood her husband's needs, but she had her own too. She was gradually becoming overwhelmed by her studies, her university activities, and her social contacts with classmates. She felt a little guilty because she really wanted to please Gaby and care for Mark Antony; she loved them both dearly and she tried her best but always felt she fell short of even her own expectations.

Gaby gave her a big party when she obtained her Master's degree. Her professors and classmates were invited as well as some of his chosen friends and colleagues. Randa was elated and felt that was the second happiest day of her life after the birth of Mark Antony. Gaby thought that he was now set to enjoy the rest of his life. What more could he ask for? A beautiful loving wife, a handsome teenage son, a promising career, a lovely home, a good circle of friends, and a sizeable and growing balance at the bank!

But no. Randa had difficulty finding a teaching position; then she found one, thank God. But then Randa had school problems: the usual ones – with colleagues, with students, with her superiors. And these were the subject of evening conversations if she was not marking papers or tests, or immersed in preparing her next day's lessons. Gaby listened, sympathized, gave advice, tried to support and help. When, thank God, these problems were solved others arose. And he had to listen and sympathize and advise and help and support. But he knew his time and hers should also be given to parenting a teenager who was passing through adolescence and who needed attention.

At school Mark Antony, with his thick, long hair, pitch-black eyes, handsome looks and a lively personality, was the focus of the girls' attention. He was doing well in his studies but he needed moral and emotional guidance, and his parents seemed to him to be absorbed in their careers and in conversations about matters or persons he cared little for. There was one particular schoolgirl he thought very highly of, and he wanted all conversation at home to be about her, but he had no chance. She was called Alexa and he liked her green eyes and shiny black hair. She was very smart in looks and dress – and her studies; and she was very friendly to him. He wanted to bring her home and present her to his parents, but he did not think they cared or had the time for that. So he went to her home, met her parents, and heard her play the piano. She enjoyed his company and he took her out to the movies and they both had fun. Was she going to be his high-school lover as his mother had been to his father? Would she later become like his mother, absorbed in herself and her career? He wondered: "Is love worth the adventure that it promises?"

Gaby was getting a little edgy and was beginning to feel the situation was approaching a possible crisis. When Randa, at the end of her second year of teaching, told him she was going back to university to study for a PhD, he hit the roof.

"A PhD degree needs at least five years of study and research, perhaps more," he thundered. "Do you think we need that?"

"I'll be much happier with a PhD and with a better teaching position at a college," she ventured.

"But our family, our son, our needs together . . . These cannot be put on hold for so long, Randa."

"They don't need to be."

"Why! Do you think Mark Antony or I enjoyed being alone doing things by ourselves when you were busy doing your MA? And do you think we've liked it during your busy school-teaching years?"

"I'm telling you, Gaby, I'm going for a PhD," Randa said firmly.

Mark Antony listened silently, then went upstairs to his room to be alone with a picture of Alexa and his thoughts.

Gaby loved Randa no less, even when she was busy with her PhD studies. But he gradually withdew from her life. He soon withdrew too from his son's life and stopped giving him those talks, which Mark Antony had liked, about his own teenage and youth experiences.

People began to notice that Gaby was seen less and less at social events, and was becoming a recluse. This affected his responsibilities at Dupont Canada Inc. He was eventually asked to resign, and received a severance pay from the company after appearing before a medical board. Even when Randa invited some of his and her friends to celebrate his birthday or some other occasion, he would sit in silence like a zombie. The only word he would utter in response to any remark or question was "Alexandria!"

Randa asked him to seek psychiatric help but he wouldn't hear of it. One day, he disappeared and left a note saying he had returned to Alexandria, but he left no address. Randa's efforts to locate him were in vain. In fact, there was no trace of him in Alexandria, and his parents, who had moved to Vancouver, knew nothing of his whereabouts. Mark Antony was disturbed. Was his mother responsible for his father's condition? What was he to do? Should he keep up his relationship with Alexa? How and where could he look for his father? Should he give his mother more time and attention? He was confused.

He was only seventeen and life seemed so complicated. There were urges within his body, thoughts in his mind, feelings in his heart. He could not think straight, and he could not understand how his mother was able to concentrate and pass her comprehensive doctoral examinations under the circumstances. He should perhaps become like her, close himself to the outside world, and focus on his studies. But there were so many beautiful things in the outside world, things to do, things to see, things to enjoy. And there was Alexa . . .

Randa was determined to complete her PhD by writing her dissertation within one year after passing the doctoral examinations. She knew this was a tall order but she also knew she could do it if she put her mind to it. Yes, she could . . . if only – if only Mark Antony would hold on and remain a good boy. Then she could start her teaching career at a college.

Little did she know that other things could impede life's progress in spite of one's having made plans. At her annual medical check-up, her doctor told her she had breast cancer. She had suspected a little lump in her breast a couple of months earlier but she was busy with her university examinations at the time and had waited for the doctor's scheduled annual check-up. He referred her to an oncologist, who confirmed her doctor's diagnosis and said the cancer was advanced and had to be operated on as soon as possible.

Then started the long days in hospital, with all kinds of tests, X-rays, drugs, injections and finally the operation. More long days followed for recuperation and exercise, and more long days with chemotherapy. Randa was exhausted and just wanted to go home. Mark Antony and her ageing parents visited her daily, and so did some of her friends. Her hospital room was full of flowers, her nurses and doctors were helpful, her visitors were all encouraging. But all she wanted was to go home and rest.

She finally did go home, only to return to hospital a few months later for further treatment. The cancer had metastasized and her treatment could have doubtful results but she was determined to have everything possible done.

Mark Antony could not hide his tears when he visited her. She hugged him as she lay there, and kissed him, saying: "Now, be strong, my boy. For my sake, be strong, and I will recover."

On his next visit he was strong. But she was not. She had lost weight, and was weak and pale. He put on a brave face and found soothing words to say to her. She smiled at him, caressed his cheek, then she asked: "Have you read Shakespeare's *Antony and Cleopatra*?"

"No," he said. "*Macbeth* was our prescribed text."

"Well, Shakespeare's tragedies were going to be the topic of my PhD dissertation, you know. I was going to study how in Shakespeare's plays love and death give meaning to life when it is too late to do anything about it."

He noticed his mother said, "I was going to study." Had she given up hope of recovering?

Randa continued: "Just before Cleopatra died by poisoning herself she remembered the love of her beloved Antony and how badly she had treated him by letting him twist in the wind and face defeat by Caesar at Actium and then commit suicide when she withdrew her fleet from supporting him. Wanting to die as a queen, Cleopatra declared:

> Give me my robe, put on my crown; I have
> Immortal longings in me. Now no more
> The juice of Egypt's grape shall moist this lip.
> Yare, yare, good Iras; quick. Methinks I hear
> Antony call; I see him rouse himself
> To praise my noble act; I hear him mock
> The luck of Caesar, which the gods give men
> To excuse their after wrath. Husband, I come:
> Now to that name my courage prove my title!
> I am fire and air; my other elements
> I give to baser life. So; have you done?
> Come then, and take the last warmth of my lips."

Her son listened and marvelled at how well versed in Shakespeare his mother was. But he wondered: Was she repentant? Did she feel she had let her husband twist in the wind? Was she now offering her son the last wisdom she could before departing this life? Is death by suicide a "noble act" as Cleopatra says? What did she mean by saying, "I have/ Immortal longings in me" or "I am fire and air"?

During the funeral service a week later, Mark Antony could not concentrate on the prayers for his mother or on the eulogy given by one of her professors at the university. His head was teeming with images of his dying mother, of his absent father, of Alexa, and his mind was crowded with questions about the meaning of life, of love, of death. His aged grandparents stood beside him to receive condolences after the burial, and he shook hands with dozens of people he knew, and with many more he did not know. It was a mechanical act, an automatic movement, a zombie-like exercise. Then Alexa shook his hand and he broke down in a paroxysm of sobs and tears.

The next thing he was conscious of was waking up, weeks later, in a pyschiatric hospital. He was served by gentle creatures in a quiet atmosphere of whiteness and sunshine, and fragrant flowers brought by his schoolmates. He was visited every day by his grandfather Antony. Little conversation passed between them at first, then after a few weeks they became chummy, until one day the doctor said that Mark Antony could go home.

Home! What home? Whose home? And to do what?

He sat in the passenger seat next to his grandfather Antony, who was driving the car home through the city of Toronto. He was told he would live with his grandparents for a while until he finished high school the following year and made arrangements for going to university.

Mark Antony remained silent. His mind, however, was astir. There was love in the world still, he thought. Life was still good, still beautiful. But it was becoming narrower, smaller and denser, and more beautiful, greatly more beautiful, because it was converging with intensity on one pretty face with glowing eyes and a radiant smile. It was the face of his high school love, it was Alexa's face, looming in front of him in the clear blue sky he saw through the car's windscreen.

When the car stopped at a red light, Mark Antony quickly jumped out, ran to the entrance of a nearby five-storey building, rushed upstairs in leaps and bounds to the roof, to the sky, and flew off to kiss the face in heaven that had launched his love.

It all happened with such speed that the grandfather was at a loss. He pulled over, parked his car round the corner, and rushed to the front door of the building.

Mark Antony's body was lying flat on the sidewalk, dead, blood oozing from his mouth. A few passers-by had collected around him, their unbelieving eyes ruefully fixed on him as on a fallen Adonis.

"Vanity of vanities; all is vanity," grandfather Antony whispered to himself as he knelt, weeping, over his grandson, while the siren of an ambulance was shrieking its way to the spot.

Search for Saleema

And finally, Khalil al-Ibrahimi died.

Nobody knows how he died. They found him after midnight, fallen on his face, in the Khan al-Zait market in the Old City of Jerusalem. Abu Saif, the night watchman of the shops, recognised him and a few Arab passers-by helped him carry the corpse to his brother's home in the dark and without noise. They all knew him and knew his story. They also knew his brother and respected him for taking good care of him for so many years. They did not want to allow the police authorities of the Israeli occupation to interfere by investigating his death, lest that should create additional problems for the family, which it could dispense with in these current conditions of the Intifada, the Palestinian uprising against the occupation. They surmised that his death was natural and caused by heart failure.

When I heard the news, the image of him when I first got to know him about twenty years ago came back into my mind. On that day, he knocked at my office door at school. The door was open and I raised my head from the reports I was writing.

He immediately said: "Good morning, sir. Would you please give me a few moments of your valuable time?"

He said that in a polite manner and in a voice full of a strange tenderness. He was tall, clean-shaven and well-dressed. He stood at the door looking at me through his glasses with affection and hope, waiting for me to permit him to enter.

I thought he was one of the students' parents, coming to ask about something or other. But I didn't recall having seen him earlier.

I said: "Please, come in."

He entered slowly and stood in front of my desk respectfully until I motioned him to a seat.

He said: "Have you seen Saleema?"

I asked: "Saleema . . . ? Who is Saleema, sir?"

He said, wondering: "Don't you know Saleema? Everybody knows Saleema. I'm surprised that you don't know Saleema."

I said: "I'm sorry. I don't know her. Saleema who?"

"Saleema Rizq," he answered seriously. "I've been looking for her since I lost her in 1948. Nineteen years have passed, and I haven't ceased asking about her and searching for her."

I began to wonder whether the man was as serious as I had thought him to be. I hastened to say something to prevent him from playing games and pulling my leg, let alone wasting my time, so I said: "I'm sorry, I don't know her, sir. Am I the mukhtar of this neighbourhood of Jerusalem to know all its inhabitants? I'm a headmaster. I have over four hundred students in my school, and they are enough for me to know by name and by face. They are more than sufficient for me to try to understand their personalities and fathom their problems; and my limited time does not even allow me to take care of them as well as I wish . . ."

He took courage and interrupted me politely: "Please, sir, forgive me. Today you're my only hope, for I spent all last night thinking whom I should ask today among the people I have not yet asked about Saleema. And I have chosen you because you know people, because you have spent many years teaching and being in the administration of this school, and you've become acquainted with the people of Jerusalem living in this neighbourhood and elsewhere, students, parents, and others. You must know someone from the family of Rizq, even if you have never been acquainted with Saleema herself."

I said: "I know individuals from the family of Razzuq, but from the family of Rizq, none. Who is Saleema Rizq, anyway? And who is she to you?"

He said anxiously, like someone drowning who has finally got hold of a rope to pull him out to safety: "She is my fiancée, sir. She is my sweetheart whom I intended and still intend to share my life with. She has a white complexion, a graceful neck, long black hair and eyes that weave radiance into love. When she speaks, her heart's tenderness and her mind's discernment are evident. And when she falls silent, beauty reigns over her and increases her charm. She is Saleema, sir. You must have seen her at work in the main post office on Jaffa Road in the last days of the British Mandate in Palestine. She was the only woman working with the public. She was twenty years old at that time and I was twenty-one, and that's when we agreed to become engaged."

He stopped talking and looked at me, expecting a response on seeing me drop the pen from my hand and on noticing some readiness on my part to reminisce. For I, too, was of his age at that time; and that beautiful young woman at the main post office used to attract my attention as she did everyone else's. And in truth, she was all tenderness and good manners. But I did not know her name and had no relation with her other than those few moments, during which I bought postage stamps from her to affix to my letters to my own fiancée, who was then a student at the American University of Beirut and who is now my wife and the mother of my children.

I nodded and said to the man: "Yes, I now remember that young lady. But I haven't seen her since those days and I don't know what happened to her."

He said: "This is my calamity, sir. I, too, haven't seen her since those days and I don't know what happened to her. And I have continued to search for her since that time."

My interest in knowing some more details grew, so I asked him: "And how did you lose her?"

He said, as if he had not earlier narrated the story one thousand and one times: "We had agreed to meet at six o'clock in the evening at the end of her office hours, so that I would accompany her to her home in Qatamon, where she lived. The people of that Arab neighbourhood in those days had begun to leave it to escape the bombs, the explosives, and the sniper bullets of the Zionists, during that last period of the British Mandate's rule when chaos was increasingly spreading in the country. The Arab fighters were becoming weaker and weaker every day, and their weapons and ammunitions were growing less and less. They were withdrawing from one section after another in Qatamon and leaving them to the Zionists. The Qatamon inhabitants moved to other Arab neighbourhoods of Jerusalem for refuge; others left the country altogether seeking safety. However, Saleema and a few others from her neighbourhood stayed put. That's why I used to accompany her daily to see her safely home.

"But she did not come to meet me that evening. So I was worried and waited for her more than an hour. Then I decided to go to Qatamon myself, after I'd ascertained that she had left the post office. She wasn't at any of the nearby hang-outs, which we sometimes frequented before she returned home. I did not find her at home, nor at any of the friends', and neighbours', homes in that beautiful

Arab suburb of Jerusalem. That night was pitch-black and terrifyingly quiet. Suddenly a loud explosion resounded nearby, illuminating the sky and shaking the ground. And lo and behold, the Semiramis Hotel was up in the air in bits and falling in ruins onto the ground, with fire breaking out in what remained of it and smoke bellowing in clouds over it. There were screams everywhere. I rushed like many others to the scene in order to help in the operations of rescuing people, giving first aid, and extinguishing the fire. I saw shocking scenes that are still present before my eyes because of their horror: disfigured corpses, bodies with terrible wounds, fragments of dead limbs, blood mixed with soil, stones piled on skulls, bones crushed under steel beams, remnants of broken furniture here and there on top of splinters of glass, porcelain shards, and broken pipes with water gushing out. All was chaos, weeping and stunned people, people who hoped for the safety of loved ones and people who had lost the dearest beings in their world, people who gave orders and people who implemented them: all gathered in the wink of an eye to lament life that was there moments before, that was snuffed out, that was smashed, that was annihilated.

"I happened to turn around when my eyes fell on the silk handkerchief I had given Saleema as a gift with her name embroidered on it. I saw it lying on the shreds of a torn carpet. I picked it up immediately and began calling Saleema repeatedly and anxiously in every corner of the ruins: Saleema, where are you, Saleema? Why didn't you wait for me, Saleema? Why did you break your promise, Saleema? Do you hear me, Saleema? Oh, Saleema! Oh, my sweetheart! Oh, Saleema!

"Someone took me aside and tried to calm me down. He remained with me until morning dawned and the rescue operations ended. No one saw any trace of Saleema. Some said she had been at the hotel, others said she had not. As for me, I don't know until now whether she was or was not. But I continue to ask everyone I see about Saleema, everyone who – I deem – knows people. Perhaps one day someone will lead me to her. She is now thirty-nine years of age. If you see her, sir, you'll recognise her: she has a white complexion, a graceful neck, long black hair and eyes that weave radiance into love. When she speaks, her heart's tenderness and her mind's discernment are evident. And when she falls silent, beauty reigns over her and increases her charm. She has fallen silent now for nineteen years."

The man suddenly stopped speaking and I saw him trying to control himself while his chin trembled and his lips quivered. I was at a loss: was he a rational person I could console or a crazy person I should cajole? And I wondered: why does love so torture us? We love a woman and all kinds of obstructions rise to face us. We love Palestine and are miserable because of this love – we love to build on its land but the enemy destroys what we build and us in the ruins. We love peace in Palestine but the enemy imposes war on us. We love life but our rightful share of it is taken by force from us. Are we a generation of victims? Who are we?

And I heard myself telling him: "I can't lead you to Saleema, my friend. But you will be led to her and will meet her one day. All you have to do is to continue searching for her and to keep the beacon of hope shining before your eyes."

The man thanked me and said: "I'm sorry, I didn't introduce myself, sir. I am Khalil al-Ibrahimi. I was an employee at the Arab Bank but was discharged some time ago because, they said, I could not concentrate on my work. I now live in the Sa'diyya quarter, in a humble home inside the Old City of Jerusalem, since we lost our beautiful villa in the Talbiyya quarter, which was occupied by the Zionists along with other Arab neighbourhoods of Jerusalem and other parts of Palestine in the Nakba, the Disaster of 1948. I now live with my elder brother, Saalim. You can get in touch with us, with him or me, if you come to know anything new about Saleema. Our telephone number is 948."

Khalil al-Ibrahimi then left my office and I have never seen him since. But I used to hear from others that he continued to ask about Saleema and search for her; he would travel from town to town in the West Bank and in the East Bank of Jordan, and would return to Jerusalem to continue his endeavours.

A few months after I had met him, the Naksa or Setback of 1967 took place. The Jordanian army withdrew from Jerusalem and the West Bank after a short war with the Israelis, in which the Palestinian fighters took part with proven bravery to no avail. Parts of Jerusalem that had been under Jordanian rule were left in ruins, including my school. So we started rebuilding and our love moved us to put together the torn fabric of our lives, even under Israeli occupation, until Arab Jerusalem stood up again on its feet, a symbol of resilience and fortitude.

Twenty-one years have now passed, during which I used to hear that the searching activities of Khalil al-Ibrahimi took him in vain to Ramla, Lydda, Jaffa, and Gaza . . . to Haifa, Acre, Nazareth, Tiberias, Bisan, and to other towns and cities of Palestine to which he could not go earlier but now had the opportunity to do so in his search for Saleema.

Then the recent Intifada began. And in this grassroots uprising of the unarmed Palestinian people against the Israeli occupation, the stones of Palestine began to speak, the stones of Palestine began to reach the conscience of people around the world. The stones of Palestine fell on the heads of Israeli soldiers, who retaliated violently with heavy arms, but they could not stop the uprising or silence its stones. And all the world saw and began to sympathise with the unjustly treated Palestinians and call for change in their situation.

I was told that Khalil al-Ibrahimi completely stopped his search for Saleema during the Intifada. And now, he finally dies in the Spring, when the Intifada is in its fifth month of vigour and he is in the sixty-first year of his life, a life most of which he spent searching for Saleema.

I wonder: Did he stop his search because he had found Saleema, that woman who has a white complexion, a graceful neck, long black hair and eyes that weave radiance into love?

I wonder: Did he die after he had found Saleema, that woman whose heart's tenderness and her mind's discernment are evident when she speaks; and when she falls silent, beauty reigns over her and increases her charm?

Did Saleema speak? Or did the stones speak for her?

Why did he stop his search for her?

Did he hear her speak? Does he hear her now?

A Retired Gentleman

Since Margaret Lutfi got married, thirty years ago, William Shibli avoided being with her alone or being seen with her alone. He even refrained from sending her birthday cards or Christmas greetings, let alone gifts or flowers, as he had done in the past. He thought she was now happily married and he should suppress any feelings for her that he had had in the past or still entertained. At social gatherings, where he occasionally saw her with Jack McConnell, her husband, he tried to make his conversation with her or him as brief as possible, and only when he could not escape it. He had established himself in the society of greater Montreal as a confirmed bachelor, whose main interest was his successful children's clothing factory.

William was now in his early seventies but, deep inside, he still felt he was only thirty. He often acted as if he were thirty indeed; for he was healthy and had retained his muscular frame, his elastic step, his erect posture, and his youthful outlook on life. He was still handsome and had a full head of hair only slightly greying. His friends knew him for his outgoing character and his coveted quality as a raconteur and a jolly, good fellow. Now a rich man living alone in a beautiful villa in Westmount with a garden, a manicured lawn, a swimming pool in the backyard and an indoor one in the basement, he continued to be for them a man of desirable company, and they all liked to be invited to his well-attended afternoon or evening parties.

When he came to Canada as a landed immigrant from Lebanon in 1950, he was twenty years old. The only child of a rather humble family, he had completed his high school education a couple of years earlier and had left Rashayya, his hometown in the southeast of Lebanon, to work in Beirut, the capital. But he was not happy with his unpromising job there and decided to emigrate to Montreal, where many of his townspeople had established themselves in businesses he heard good things about. In Montreal, he worked as a sales manager for an older, distant relative of his who owned a womenswear factory. A few years later, he felt he knew the ins and outs of the business and was confident to start his own. The Royal Bank of Canada gave him a loan and he established his Children's Clothing Company, later famously known in the market as CCC, with its 250 workers and forty years of commercial success. His business benefited first from the post-war baby boom and then from the provincial government's policy of encouraging families of Quebec to have more children by offering family allowances to mothers.

A multimillionaire at age sixty-five, he decided in 1995 to retire and wanted to sell his business. He had several offers but the best one was from a Jewish businessman, who had been his main competitor. Some of his Arab friends in the Montreal apparel business advised him against it, mainly under the influence of political considerations in support of Palestinians who, under Israeli occupation, were fighting for their liberation and a separate state of their own. He gave the matter some thought but finally decided to go ahead and ignore his friends' advice. He argued that those friends themselves continued to trade with the thread factories in Montreal owned mostly by Jews, who virtually monopolized the thread that everyone in the apparel industry needed. Besides, he believed that in Canada everyone had an equal opportunity.

And so, William Shibli became a retired gentleman. He had not gone back to Lebanon even once for a visit since his migration to Canada, but he often thought of his old country, especially as it was constantly in the news during its fifteen-year uncivil war that started in 1975, followed by the Israeli invasion of Lebanon in 1982 and the continuing fighting against Israeli domination in the south of the country. He contributed money to St. Nicholas Orthodox Church in Rashayya and to specific poor persons in his hometown parish; he also made donations to charitable groups assisting displaced families in Lebanon, and to groups sponsoring and helping Lebanese refugees in Canada. He wanted to alleviate people's miseries and did his best to keep his good works anonymous.

In his retirement, he spent a long time remembering his past, especially the first twenty years of his life in Lebanon, but also his later days in Canada, as he sat alone at home listening to music or watching the birds and enjoying the flowers in his garden or looking at old photographs of his family and friends, many of whom had departed this life, including his own parents. Occasionally he gave parties to his friends, and his servants liked the atmosphere of conviviality that these parties brought to his usually quiet home. He took up playing golf once a week and continued his routine of daily swimming. He also took a fancy to the recently developed internet and to correspondence with his friends by email. He never felt lonely, his memory and imagination being his inseparable companions when human company was not available.

He remembered the olden days with Margaret back in Rashayya and the beautiful experiences of adolescent, innocent love they both had. He remembered the long walks he took with her in the fields, in the orchards, and in the olive groves as well as the endless conversations about nothing. He remembered the games they played with other youths of Rashayya and the dabka dances they danced at weddings and other festive occasions. He remembered the gnawing jealousy he felt when Margaret spoke with other young men and he pretended not to care. He remembered the pain he felt when she played hard to get, when she did not want to go for a walk with him, and especially when she once devastated him by going for a walk with another young man. Now he smiles, how innocent those experiences were! Yet how deeply genuine and true, and how beautiful! Oh yes, and he still remembered how sweet that first kiss of Margaret had been!

One spring day, when their relationship was at its best, William said: "Margaret, let's go to Mount Hermon. That will be the longest walk we've ever taken together."

She replied: "It's a long way, William . . ."

He said: "A few hours' walk. We'll take water and sandwiches with us. We can do it and we'll enjoy it."

"What will people say?" she cautioned.

"Let them say what they want. They won't see us, any-way."

She looked at him, lovingly, then at Mount Hermon looming on the southern horizon of Rashayya, with its eternally snow-clad top. It appeared like the hoary head of an old man, a venerable hermit watching Rashayya and the docile countryside it towered.

She finally agreed: "All right, William. Let's go."

It was on this walk that he told her he was leaving Rashayya. They had reached the foot of Mount Hermon and he suggested that they should rest before the ascent to the snowy summit. They chose a shady place facing north toward Rashayya, which was bathed in haze at a distance.

He asked her: "You haven't been to Beirut, have you, Margaret?"

She said: "No. But I'd like to visit it one day."

He asked: "Would you like to live there . . . with me?"

"With you!? . . ." she exclaimed.

"Yes, I'm going to Beirut to work there."

She hesitated then said: "No, I can't go with you." Then she added, with innocent youthful wisdom: "Unless we're married . . ."

William replied: "You know I love you, Margaret, and I intend to marry you. I thought we were agreed on that. But since I have no certainty of income yet, I cannot marry you immediately."

"Oh, what an unlucky girl I am," she sighed. Trying to suppress her tears, she finally added bravely: "Go to Beirut, William, but do keep in touch, you hear me? . . . I'll wait."

Margaret then grumbled she could not go uphill to the mountain top and wanted to return home. And William still remembered how sad and how much longer that almost silent return home seemed to be.

A couple of years later, William returned to Rashayya from Beirut, but only to tell Margaret he was emigrating to Canada. She cried and sobbed on his shoulder, and did not believe his promise that he would bring her over to Canada and marry her as soon as he became financially in a position to do so.

After his departure, she immediately began to make her own plans to go to Canada to be with him, and she succeeded in accompanying her uncle, who was also going as a landed immigrant. In Montreal, she went to McGill University to finish her education in history while William was working for a distant relative of his. She continued to see him now and then, but he was usually too busy with his sales duties and even busier when he later started his own children's clothing factory. His gifts to her, his flowers, his birthday and Christmas cards could not replace moments of intimacy she craved for but could not have.

Meanwhile, Margaret began to have a liking for Jack McConnell, an engineering student she met at several social activities of the Students' Society at McGill University. She increasingly enjoyed being with him at parties of various fraternities. And before you knew it, Margaret got married to Jack McConnell after they graduated. Jack was immediately hired by Bombardier Inc., one of Quebec's biggest engineering firms, and he and Margaret led a happy married life, recently celebrating their thirtieth wedding anniversary.

William Shibli was retired for over five years now and had adapted himself to the routine of a quiet life, pleasant pastimes, and occasional social functions. One of the pastimes that had really grown on him was his email correspondence with friends. However, one of his most interesting email correspondents was a graduate student at

McGill University's Faculty of Management who had obtained his email address from her professor and introduced herself as Lena McConnell, studying for a Master's degree in business administration. The name immediately rang a bell but her research project on the Montreal garment industry of the Arab immigrant community intrigued William, and he determined to give her all the help she asked for. He had never met her and became increasingly interested in meeting her as the days went by and as she showed a growing knowledge of the industry she was researching.

At the beginning, her email messages were short and mostly in the form of questions sent once a week. She wanted first to know of the experience of "Mr Shibli" in the field, how he started, how his business developed, and how he thought he achieved his success. She also wanted to learn about his competitors in the industry, what he thought of them, and how he dealt with them. Then, at her request, he arranged for her to visit several of the clothing factories of his friends in town. Her email messages became more frequent and now arrived every other day, then almost daily, and she asked more knowledgeable, technical questions about supply and demand, purchases and sales, resources and raw materials, labour relations and wages, advertising and publicity, profits and losses. Her questions about his past experience in the actual production of goods in his own children's clothing factory came a few weeks later, and she asked about graphic artists and designers, sewing and cutting machines, pattern-making, needlework, grading and quality control, packaging, division of labour and ranks of workers. She also asked about the impact of government labour laws on the business, the evident lack of unionization among workers, the proportion of men to women in the labour force and their relative wages. Then she wanted to know ("if possible") about his personal relations as a male employer with his workers of both sexes. She said she had come to know that, in the Montreal garment industry, most workers were women, the men being only a few in each firm and usually working as sales managers, accountants, machine repairmen, shippers and truck drivers.

At that point in his correspondence with Lena McConnell, William Shibli decided to invite her to his home so that, as he told her, he might become personally acquainted with her and answer all her remaining questions before she wrote up her thesis. He was not sure she would accept his invitation and was surprised to find that she was more than eager to meet him.

At ten o'clock in the morning of the appointed spring day, she appeared at his doorstep: a lovely young lady in her mid-twenties, tall and slim, wearing tight blue jeans, a white blouse with long flared sleeves, and a red silk scarf around her neck knotted on the left side. Her short, dark brown hair framed her face with two curves on her cheeks almost meeting at her chin, and her smile made her honey-colored eyes shine even more brightly. She carried a writing-pad in a folder. William shook her hand and asked her if she did not mind sitting by the swimming pool in the backyard.

"No. That'll be lovely," she said. "It's a beautiful day."

"We'll have tea there. Or would you like coffee?"

"Tea is fine," she said as she allowed him to lead her to the pool.

They both sat at a white, wrought-iron table under a large white and yellow umbrella, and a maid soon brought a silver tea set as they were engaged in conversation.

William felt he knew this young lady very well and was comfortable being with her. On her part, she felt equally comfortable talking to him after several months of email correspondence, in which she had lately addressed him as "Dear William" or "My very dear William" or "Dearest William". He was more than four decades older than she was but he felt she strengthened within him a consciousness that he was her age by the way she spoke to him. He sensed that her respect for him was infused with a great measure of admiration. And judging from his kind voice and sympathetic attention, she felt that his interest in her was inspired by a lot of tenderness and affection.

Little did they know that their admiration and affection were to last a lifetime and that they would become an unusual twosome. For that meeting of theirs was followed by others, then by going together to the movies and restaurants, and by attending together Les Grands Ballets Canadiens de Montréal in a subscription to their year-long ballet programme at the city's Place des Arts. William Shibli bore all the expenses, of course, but he could not prevent Lena McConnell from buying him a present for his birthday, a lovely silk tie he always wore with pride and his usual panache.

He felt he was living the best days of his life after Lena had become his friend and almost constant companion. His friends noticed his diminished attention to them; even his email contacts with them became sparse and tepid. Many of them saw him with Lena in town and wondered about his relationship with her, but in the end discovered that it was utterly above board. His servants at home accepted Lena's frequent presence but always asked politely whether she would be expected at any of the day's meals when the dining table was about to be set.

On her part, Lena was also happy with William's pleasant companionship and affection, which did not deter her in any way from keeping up her friendly relationship with young men at her school, and with one particular boyfriend she liked. She was mature enough to appreciate William's care and kindness and to develop a deep and warm feeling for him in her heart. In her emails that she continued to send him when they did not meet, she often signed off with "I send you my love" or "With all my love" or "Much love" or simply "Love." At first, William did not know what to make of these sign-offs, for as a man who still retained Arab values, he associated love with marriage and sex, and these were far from his mind in his relationship with Lena. In his emails to her, he signed off with "Your sincere friend" or "Your friend who cherishes you infinitely" or "With deep affection" or simply "Affectionately". Later on, when he caught on to Lena's Canadian language and signed off with "Love" or, more bravely "With all my love", he felt elated but deep down he felt he was somehow betraying Margaret, his first and only love of half a century.

One morning at the beginning of autumn, when the leaves had turned and the trees were a glorious sight of blending colours, Margaret came to see him at home without any prior arrangement. The maid showed her into the drawing room to wait for him. When he came downstairs from his bedroom, the air became redolent of the fresh fragrance of the Parisian eau de cologne he was wearing as he greeted Margaret amiably, hiding his deep surprise.

This was the first time since her marriage that William had seen her in private. She stood up and shook his hand.

"I'm sorry I've come without prior notice," she began as they both sat down near the fireplace. "But I hope you don't mind, William."

"Not at all, Margaret," he said, trying to put her at ease.

"Well, you see, it's about Lena," she continued. "I've only recently learned of her relationship with you."

"Oh . . ."

"You know Lena is my daughter."

"She never told me but I suspected it all along. And I didn't want to bring it up with her because I felt she did not want me to, and she seemed to have her reasons."

"She's my only child, you know, and I'm worried about her infatuation with you. She has told me how you've helped her immensely in gathering information for her Master's thesis, and I'm grateful to you. She speaks so highly of you and keeps reminding Jack and me that she'll invite you to her graduation ceremony at McGill's convocation next spring."

"It will be my honour to be present at her graduation. She's a clever and mature young lady and I respect her a lot. As for her special relationship with me, I don't think there's anything to worry about, Margaret. It's not 'infatuation', as you put it; it's rather real friendship, which I appreciate very, very much and am determined not to lose, for it makes her and me happy."

"But don't you think it's going beyond the bounds of usual friendship when you and she spend so much time together . . . considering the difference in age between you? . . ."

"No, Margaret. And age has nothing to do with it. This is real friendship, real appreciation of each other's company," William said firmly.

"Do you mean you don't love her?"

"Of course, I love her. But I'm not in love with her, as I was with you." Then William summoned up his courage and added: "You may not believe this, but I still love you, Margaret, and I don't think anyone will ever take your place in my heart."

Margaret was taken aback and flustered as she stood up and muttered: "Oh, William. What an unlucky girl I was and what a stupid and silly woman I am now!"

William went up to her to comfort her. She put up her arms to him and he hugged her and patted her back gently. Then he looked into her eyes . . . and their lips met in a warm, long-desired kiss.

Then he let go of her and said, stiffly: "This has never happened. Please go home to your family, Margaret."

"I should have gone up with you to the summit of Mount Hermon . . . Oh, William. I should have waited for you in Rashayya, I should have waited for you in Montreal too. . . I still love you, William . . ."

Looking away, he said: "I've not heard that . . ."

Then, moments later, he took out a key from his pocket, gave it to her, and said: "Please, open the safe behind that painting on the wall."

Still flustered and confused, Margaret opened the safe and, as directed, she took out the top document and began to read it.

It was a copy of William's will. Upon his death, the American University of Beirut was to receive, by a previously signed agreement, one million dollars to establish a Shibli Chair for Business Administration. As for the balance of his estate, including his villa in Westmount, he was bequeathing it to Lena McConnell "in appreciation and friendship," and further "in recompense for her pleasant companionship over a long time".

As William took back the document and placed it in the safe, he said: "Please, Margaret. Don't breathe a word about this to Lena or anyone else."

"I won't," she said. "But I have told her about our own love story, long ago. I hope you don't mind?"

"She never told me anything about that," he said. Then he added: "Why did you call her Lena, I always wondered?"

She said, "Lena, as you know, is a diminutive of Magdalene – Mary Magdalene, that is. When Lena was born, we gave her this name because Jack and I liked it on account of the pure love it symbolizes, the deep pure love between Mary Magdalene and Jesus."

"This says it all," he said. "This is the love, the real friendship, between Lena and myself."

Margaret's eyes were welling up with tears, and so were William's. However, he composed himself and managed to say: "Please go home, Margaret. Take care of your family, and take good care of Lena for me."

True Love, Mad Love

She knew I was Jim's best friend and that I knew of his deep affection for her. When the tragedy of his death came to be known and many thought she was responsible for his rash act, she did her best to justify herself and began to speak to everyone who knew both of them, to explain that she still loved Jim and missed him terribly, now irretrievably, and that she had done nothing to deserve blame for his suicide and the accusations currently prevalent among his friends. To me, she gave a copy of his last letter to her and I was baffled on reading it. I could not make up my mind and decided to ask you, my friends and his, what you think.

So, here is Jim's last letter to Nadia, after which he apparently lived a normal life for more than a year, as all his San Francisco friends and acquaintances attest. Please read it and let me know what you think, and relieve me of my uncertainty.

Thanks.

San Francisco,
25 June, 2001

Dear Nadia,

Let me for a while fantasize. I hope you have the time to read this letter. Suppose you did not send me your latest email message. I will then have come to Boston to see you, having known that you are now back home from Florida. I will ring your doorbell. You will open the door and unexpectedly see me standing there with a bouquet of flowers. What will you do?

I have a feeling you will not recognize me at first. But having seen me once for a few minutes at an Arab-American poetry reading in Washington, DC a year ago and having later seen my picture, you will remember the hundreds of words we exchanged since then, by correspondence and on the telephone, and you will collect yourself together and say, "Jimmeee! Come in, come in. You're here from San Francisco. Shame on you! Why didn't you tell me you were coming?"

I will enter. Your apartment is in a mess. "Forgive this

mess, Jim," you will say. "I returned from Florida only yesterday and I've had no time yet to tidy up."

I will say: "Nadia, I've come to see you, forget about the mess. How are you, my friend? How's your family in Florida?"

"I'm fine, and they're fine too," you will say, still trying to collect a few things strewn all over, then you take the flowers from me and put them in a vase.

"Nadia, please come and sit down next to me."

"Let me first turn the kettle on, and we can have coffee . . . and more coffee. And we'll talk and plan our day."

You return from the kitchen and sit by me, smiling and looking me over.

"Here we are together at last, after a whole year," you say.

I agree: "Here we are together at last. What shall we do together? I'm staying at the Hilton Hotel, in downtown Boston, and I'm planning to stay two days. I'm on my way to New York, where I will lecture at Columbia University. My friend Professor Meagan Nowell at Columbia invited me to speak on Arab-American poets, and I jumped at the opportunity . . ."

"What an opportunity!" you remark. "What will you say about Arab-American poets?"

I'll say: "Nadia Asaly is my favorite, but I have to say why. As you know, there are well-established poets like Etel Adnan, D H Melhem, Samuel Hazou, Naomi Shihab Nye, Elmaz Abi-Nader, Gregory Orfalea, Lisa Suhair

Majaj, Nathalie Handal, Paul Nassar, Mohja Kahf, Khaled Mattawa, and a dozen others, who are accomplished and well-published poets, some of them having earned prestigious awards in America. So I can't just begin with Nadia Asaly. But I will build up my argument and will lead to you as one of the youngest and most innovative . . . I mean, one of the most creative poets and one with a most fertile imagination. Your poems are dreams, Nadia, unattached to everyday reason. Like dreams, they grow, scene after scene without logical links except for the powerful force of the vivid imagination pouring out one image after another so that, in the end, the cumulative picture coming out will itself be the poem – the dream . . ."

You listen. I stop talking. I look at you, admiringly. Your face shines. Your eyes sparkle. I smile and say: "Nadia, I haven't come to lecture you, my dear. I've come to see you, to speak to you, to listen to you, to do things with you, to be with you."

You say: "Go on. I like your words and your warm voice, I like to hear you talk, to see your hands expressing your thoughts before your mouth utters the words, I like to watch your eyes as they twinkle at every thought and I can see through them into the deepest part of your soul, your beautiful soul that I admire so much because it evokes Arabian romances and their mysteries . . ."

The kettle whistles. "Oh, I have to get the coffee," you say, rising. "I have some date-chip cookies that Mom

made and gave me in Florida, following Grandma's Palestinian recipe. Would you like to have some with your coffee?"

"Sure."

You come back with coffee for two and your mother's
date-chip cookies.

"Listen," you begin. "Let's go out after coffee. We'll
walk and walk in the Back Bay area and along the bank of
the Charles River for a while, then at noon we'll go to a
French restaurant I like and we'll have lunch there with
Bordeaux wine. How about that?"

"Fine."

"In the evening," you continue, " we'll go to a play or
a movie then we'll have dinner at another French restaurant I like, and more French wine. Then coffee . . . and
more coffee. I'm not suggesting one of the Arab restaurants because you have so many of them in San Francisco."

"Fine, Nadia. What we need is to talk and talk all the
time . . ."

"Indeed, Jim. This is a short visit but we'll make the
most of it."

I drink my coffee. I look at you, I enjoy being with
you, and in my heart I hope the moments in your company will keep rolling on and on, endlessly. Then I say:
"Yes, let's make the most of it. Are you ready to go out?"

You disappear for a few moments into your bedroom
then come out in a grey skirt, a white blouse, and a blue

jacket and wearing a red and black flowered scarf around your neck. You are as elegant as can be.

"I'm ready," you say blithely. "Let's go."

Then we leave your apartment together.

To be in Boston with Nadia – my dream, your poem!

★ ★ ★

No, Nadia. This is not what happened. This is not what will happen, either. You know very well that what happened was totally different. Why should you or anyone suppose that I came to Boston to see you and that I actually did see you? You know how much I love you, Nadia. But you don't seem to know how consumed I am by your love, how devoted I am to the idea of loving you. This idea is inhabiting my whole being, Nadia. It's obsessing me day and night. I keep thinking of nothing and of no one but you, as though thinking about you will bring you to me in the flesh, and then I can see you, touch you, talk to you, listen to you, laugh with you, and feel as free as a bird like I do when I am with you.

No, that is not what happened, Nadia, and you know it. So what use is it to you to send you this letter and repeat to you what actually happened, when you and I know what really did happen? Yet, I dare to repeat to you what happened, only so it may sink down into your consciousness as I think it did not when it actually happened the first time. You are so carefree, Nadia. You are as light-hearted as a butterfly, and you keep going from one notion to another as a butterfly goes from one flower to another, without thought, without care, without any interest in what your movements do to the man who wishes you would stay with him long enough for one notion, for one idea, for one feeling, and perhaps then you would make him happy or, at least, he would feel happy.

What really happened, Nadia, is that I did not come to see you in Boston. I only sent you an email message saying I was coming to Boston. As I told you, I am very busy preparing my lecture to be given at Columbia University; but the moment I learned that you were back in Boston, I left my lecture preparations to be done during the flight from San Francisco to Boston. I thought I could do that, spend two days in Boston for further research, spend a couple of hours with you and then go to New York and give my lecture. But, no. That was not what happened. That was not what was destined to happen. Why? Because you immediately sent me an email message in reply, saying you could not see me because you were not able to free yourself to see me.

Not able to free yourself to see me . . .?!

Look at me, freeing myself of all my important commitments in order to come to Boston to see you. And look at you, unable to free yourself to see me. And what is your excuse, pray? If it were death in the family, God forbid, I would understand. If it were a medical appoint-

ment with a strict physician who required six months'
notice for appointments, I would also understand. Even
if it were a meeting with your publisher, who was considering your love poems and wanted to see your friend's
paintings that would accompany them, I would also
understand. But you said you could not see me because
you were busy and overworked, because you were not in
the mood on account of your concerns and worries over
your investments that were not doing well on the stock
market, because you were tired and needed rest. Well,
ALL I needed was an hour or two with you, Nadia.

Why don't you say you don't love me any more? That
would be more honest and straightforward, and I could
understand that. You once said: "Love is fragile, Jim." You
also said: "If the flame of love dies down, one should let
it go, for there will be other flames." I understand all this
philosophy of ephemeral love, although my love is not
like that. Mine is a true Arab love that clings and does not
let go. But what galls me is that you always said to me
during our year-long correspondence: "You are beautiful," "You have a generous spirit," "You are sweet," "I
think about you always," and "You are and will always be
in my heart." And in the American way you always ended
your email messages "With all my love, always". Always?
Always?! How long is "always" in your love dictionary?
How stable and firm is "being" in your heart, Nadia?
How steadfast is your love? Am I your first love, your
tenth, your hundredth? You constantly said that I was the

first, that there was no one like me. You always ended your telephone calls by saying "I love you". And I believed you because I needed to believe you in order to make you happy, for I loved you too and had come to accept you and accept my lot in life with you. You have been part of my life, even through correspondence and telephone calls, and my hope has been that we would soon agree to be together for ever.

This is what happened, Nadia. You have broken my heart. I was in love with you, and the flame of our love was burning bright but you did not care to keep it bright by seeing me for one hour or two. To my Arab way of thinking, love is not fragile when two people work on it to keep it alive. Love is a splendid experience, Nadia. It is a wonderful miracle that gives human beings a winged life to be free, to be above all the cares of this world: physicians, investments, publishers, overwork, exhaustion, whatever. Love is the balm that soothes our concerns and worries, that allays our fears and uncertainties, that heals our wounds, that erases our loneliness in this world, that unites us and makes us able to face life, and teaches us to give and give and give. In love, we don't lose when we give, nor do we gain when we take. In true love, there is joy in giving all the time. Taking is never thought of, the lover takes what the beloved freely gives as a recognition of the beloved.

"Don't come," you said. "It is not a good idea. We can plan to see each other later and I will send you another email message about this."

Thank you, Nadia, I appreciate the fact that you replied. In this you are truly American, and I respect that. But I am writing to let you know that I am through with correspondence, email and airmail alike, I am through with telephone calls. Thanks, but no thanks, Nadia. I will keep you as an idea in my mind, a beautiful idea I will always cherish. I will always remain devoted to my beautiful idea of loving you.

I will fly directly to New York from San Francisco and I will give my lecture at Columbia University. I will speak about your poetry, about your images and dreams, about your innovative ideas and vivid imagination. But that is all I will do, that is all I can do. Then I will return to San Francisco to carry on with my life, alone and in love with the beautiful idea of loving you. Crazy, perhaps? A Majnun Layla in America, perhaps? Some people may think so. Not I, for that is who I am. And you've always said you like who I am. I am your loving friend who will not see you but will keep his sanity.

Jim

Literary Influences

Books and I

The first book I ever read by myself from cover to cover in one sitting was an Arabic one entitled *The Little Red Hen*. I was about eight years old in 1937, a pupil in the third elementary class at a government school in Jerusalem during the British Mandate of Palestine. The joy I felt during the weekly hour in Sitt Wasila's class devoted to silent reading of Arabic books she distributed to her pupils was ineffable and is still with me to this day. Little did I know then that that was the opening for me to the endless world of literature.

I had learned to read Arabic in *Al-Jadid*, the popular and extensively used series of four reading books (Jerusalem, 1924–1933) by the great Palestinian educator and author Khalil Sakakini (1878–1953). Right from the first page of Book One, I learned to read the words *ras* and *rus* (meaning 'head' and 'heads' as the illustration showed), and on the second page *dar* and *dur* (meaning 'house' and 'houses' as the illustration also showed) using an additional letter to those learned earlier, and so on to the end of the book, which culminated in teaching the Arabic alphabet from reading the names of illustrated everyday things seen and experienced by the pupils, and without learning it abstractly as single letters arrayed in a specific order. Book Two introduced simple sentences and easy grammatical structures, using daily conversation; and Books Three and Four elaborated by offering further simple readings and brief stories, without the insipid rules of traditional grammars.

Hence, I could easily read and enjoy *Al-Dajaja al-Saghira al-Hamra' (The Little Red Hen)* in the third elementary class and, later, many other similarly delightful books in the weekly silent hour of Sitt Wasila's class. But imagine my great surprise and delight on seeing Khalil Sakakini himself in my class one day. He was paying an official visit to my school as the government's Inspector of Arabic. He was a strongly-built man, tall and portly and awe-inspiring. He wore a red fez and had a commanding and dignified presence. His eyes shone brilliantly with intelligence, and an encouraging smile never abandoned his lips. He spoke in classical Arabic and I was asked by Sitt Wasila to read a text to him. I read it aloud, trying to conceal my nervousness and slight intimidation. When I finished, he asked for the meaning of the word *fawran* that I had read in the text. No one in the class knew, so he used it in a sentence and asked again for its meaning. I raised my hand with a few other students but he did not call on any of us. He used the word *fawran* in another sentence and asked for its meaning again. More students now raised their hands to answer. But he did not call on any of them until he gave a third sentence using the same word again. At that moment, almost all the students raised their hands eager to answer, and those asked said – correctly – it meant 'immediately'.

I admired Khalil Sakakini and wanted to be like him when I grew up, a good teacher and educator with an excellent knowledge of Arabic language and literature. I later learned that he was the author of more than a dozen books; that he was an indomitable man whose participation in Palestinian politics in Ottoman and British times often led to his imprisonment; that he always cherished freedom and dignity and truth and justice as essential human values worth struggling for; that he had a good sense of humour, was interested in music, played the violin, and liked good food and a hearty life enhanced by physical exercise and sports; that at different times of his life, he was a member of a variety of literary circles in Jerusalem which gathered the best Arab intellectuals and writers of the day for informal conversations which were a pleasure to attend; that he had friends among the writers of other parts of the Arab world and was in contact with them; and that he was elected as a member of the prestigious Academy of the Arabic Language in Cairo.

Of his books which I later read, I liked in particular two very personal books: firstly, his book *Sari* (Jerusalem,

1935) in which he gathered all the letters he had sent from Jerusalem to his son Sari who was at university in USA between 1931 and 1935; and secondly, his book *Li-Dhikraki* (*In Your Memory*, Jerusalem, 1940) in which he poured out his heart at the death of his beloved wife Sultana in 1940 for whom he had written his best poetry earlier. While many Arabs would rather keep such personal feelings and thoughts private, Khalil Sakakini made his public, strongly believing that the best literature is written about the genuine inner experiences of a human being, expressed beautifully to display the impact of living on him and to wonder at the meaning of life. His other book that I also liked was his posthumously published memoirs *Kadha Ana, Ya Dunya* (*Such Am I, O World*, Jerusalem, 1955) in which he opened himself to be fully known as he passed through life, recording his various experiences, his thoughts, and his feelings without reservation. The book is not only a frank register of his life but also of Palestine, its society, its people and its intellectuals, and is written as if consciously addressed to history so that all may know the point of view of the uniquely untraditional person he was, who always yearned courageously and outspokenly for something new and better, and disliked being bound by conventions. "Such am I, O world," he told history, using the very words of the heroic and ebullient classical Arab poet he liked most, Abu al-Tayyib al-Mutanabbi (915–965).

After the 1948 Nakba, he lost his home in Qatamon,

one of the most beautiful Arab neighbourhoods of Jerusalem, to the Zionist fighters; his belongings were savagely plundered and his library was barbarously looted, and he had to flee for his life and his family's, and take refuge in Cairo for some time. Then I briefly saw him afterwards in the Old City of Jerusalem, which had come under Jordan's rule after the rest of Jerusalem and much of Palestine had come under Israel's, following the 1948 war at the end of the British Mandate. A fallen titan, a broken old man, his dignity still bristled; the shine in his eyes had dimmed a little but he still believed that justice would eventually prevail and truth would always triumph. The streak in his thinking that had begun in the latter part of his life to favour the poetry and thought of the pessimistic and sceptic classical Arab poet Abu al-'Ala' al-Ma'arri (973-1058) had become stronger in him. He did not live much longer after that, and he died in 1953.

* * *

When in 1938 I completed the third elementary class, which was the highest in my school, my father did not want me to continue my education in the free government school system. He sent me to complete my schooling at the Collège des Frères, a private high school established in 1878 in the Old City of Jerusalem and run by the Christian Brothers, an internationally known Catholic teaching order, who were helped by a number of non-clerical teachers. It charged high fees, but my father wanted me to have the advantage at it of learning French and English in addition to Arabic, and of benefiting from its distinguished curriculum and possibly from its famous discipline. The change to a boys' school with male teachers after my earlier schooling at a co-educational school with female teachers was a little disrupting, but I quickly adapted myself to it, despite the daily attendance of mass and catechism classes compulsory for all Christian students, the Muslim students and the few Jews being exempted. The school day was longer and fully occupied with intensive courses, except for a mid-morning break and a mid-afternoon break of fifteen minutes each, and a lunch break of one hour.

What I missed greatly was the silent hour of Sitt Wasila with her interesting, colourful books. My new school had a library, but it consisted of locked glass bookcases hung along one wall in the long corridor of the school's second floor in three sections: Arabic, English, and French. It had no catalogue, not even a list of its books which never seemed to increase in number. The Brother responsible for it unlocked one of its bookcases for a few minutes once a week and gave the eager students who cared to come and swarm around him what he selected for them to borrow and read. I was usually the first to arrive. After several years, I thus came to read many of the Arabic books of Kamel Kilani for children and young adults, mostly graded and simplified books in large print and with pictures, based on selected (and expurgated) stories from the *One Thousand and One Nights* and on other Arabic classics, but also adventure stories adapted from Western literatures like Daniel Defoe's *Robinson Crusoe*, Jonathan Swift's *Gulliver's Travels*, Robert Louis Stevenson's *Treasure Island*, and Cervantes' *Don Quixote*. Noticing I was an avid and rather more advanced reader, Frère Epiphane, the Lebanese Brother responsible for the Arabic bookcases, slipped me more than one book per week. When I was in my early teens, he selected for me Arabic historical novels to read and especially those of Jurji Zaydan (1861–1914), which I enjoyed because they taught me Arab history while entertaining my inquisitive mind. Arab history was shamefully deficient in the school's curriculum, and so was geography. Pretty soon, I was surfeited with the books the school 'library' could offer, and I needed richer and more satisfying readings, when I was lucky to fall upon a treasure trove at home.

★ ★ ★

It was a collection of Arabic books and magazines that belonged to my father in the 1920s and 1930s and that were kept in a crate under a couch. He was a civil servant in the government of the British Mandate: a superintendent of the Telegraph Office in Jerusalem at one time, and a postmaster later. As a younger man and freer then of family and work responsibilities, he used to read widely in his leisure time. Overworked and latterly bedridden with rheumatoid arthritis, he had little interest in reading; but he gladly let me read his collection and took pleasure in discussing my readings with him. To me, this was even better than Sitt Wasila's reading hour of my childhood, for I was now intellectually blossoming in the secondary classes at school in the middle 1940s, and he was a very knowledgeable guide and a most loving mentor to me. To him I owe a great measure of my literary orientation.

Prominent in the collection were some of the books of Gibran Khalil Gibran (1883–1931), of whom my father was an admirer. His *The Prophet*, rendered into Arabic by Archimandrite Antonios Bashir (d. 1966), was my introduction to Gibran's contemplative thought and lyrical style, which immediately charmed me. This charm was further reinforced by reading his *Dam'a wa Ibtisama* (*A Tear and a Smile*, 1914), *Al-Arwah al-Mutamarrida* (*Spirits Rebellious*, 1908), and *Al-Bada'i' wa al-Tara'if* (*Wonders and Curiosities*, 1923). Fascinated by Gibran's poetic prose style and by his rebellion against social conventions and his defence of the downtrodden, I later read all his works wherever I found them, and I even pursued the works of all his colleagues in the Pen Bond of New York which he led, especially those of Mikhail Naimy, Iliyya Abu Madi, 'Abd al-Masih Haddad, and Nasib 'Arida.

Another book in my father's collection was *Al-'Abarat* (*Tears*, 1915) by Mustafa Lutfi al-Manfaluti (1879–1924), a collection of sad stories that he adapted from Western literature. An Azhar graduate, he clung to a traditional prose style which oddly conveyed a melancholy romantic mood bordering on sentimental pessimism. I later read more of his books elsewhere but did not take to him.

A different author was Anatole France (1844–1924), and my father's collection had two of his novels: *Thaïs* and *Le Lys Rouge*, translated into Arabic by Muhammad al-Sawi Muhammad. Even in the Arabic translation, the pure and limpid language of this 1921 Nobel laureate and master of literary style came through. I liked him and later read in French some of his other books including his *Le Crime de Sylvestre Bonnard*; I admired his satiric tone and delicate irony, and I learned from him what a subtle and powerful tool language can be.

Not so was the style of another book in my father's collection: *Les Amants de Venise* by Michel Zevaco, translated into Arabic as *'Ushshaq Finisiya* by someone whose name I don't even remember. Nor so was the style of another translated novel on Pope Alexander VI (Rodrigo Borgia) telling about his political and ecclesiastical intrigues and his many mistresses and children. Although I appreciated the fact that he patronised great artists like Raphael and Michelangelo, I don't think he ever made me forgive his misuse of office, but rather made me ever wary of people in high positions.

Books of a totally different nature in my father's collection had a great influence on my thinking; they were by Salama Musa (1887–1958), the Egyptian liberal thinker and moderniser who, while studying in England, adopted the socialist philosophy of the Fabian Society and propounded it in his Arabic writings. Of his other writings, I read his book *Nazariyyat al-Tatawwur wa Asl al-Insan*, popularising Darwin's theory of evolution, and I have ever since supported this theory and concurred with its more recent scientific findings; likewise, I have supported Salama Musa's feminist views and his call for an Arabic literature of free ideas and simple style addressed to the common people, not to the elite.

The Arabic magazines in my father's collection were incomplete series of well-known monthlies, most of which dealt with topics similar to those above. They included *Al-Hilal* of Jurji Zaydan (which was historical, literary, and general), *Al-Muqtataf* of Ya'qub Sarruf and Fares Nimr (which was scientific and general), *Minerva* of Mary Yanni (which was feminist, literary, and general), and *Al-Nafa'is al-'Asriyya* of the Jerusalemite Khalil Baidas (which was fiction-oriented and published literary translations, especially from Russian fiction). There was also *Al-Riyada al-Badaniyya* specialising in medical information and health, and it included sexology in which, as a teenager, I was extremely interested. These and other magazines opened for me monthly contacts with Arab writers and intellectuals from Egypt, Lebanon, Syria, Iraq, and Palestine. I was certain the Christian Brothers at my school would not approve of my readings, but I did not let that thought deter me.

★ ★ ★

When my father's crate of books had nothing more to offer me, I came to know a much larger crate that contained over 50,000 books and periodicals. That was the library of the YMCA. I was in my last three years of secondary school in 1944–1947 when I joined the YMCA and was more eager than ever to read and have social contacts with a larger world. The Christian Brothers forbade their Catholic students to join this Protestant institution; but since I was an Orthodox Christian Arab, I was free to join and I did, despite my school's discouragement. I never regretted this act, for in addition to athletics at the YMCA, I made new friends and a new world opened up for me in the public lectures, the art exhibits, the musical concerts, and occasional plays I could attend there. No one ever tried to make me a Protestant at the YMCA, as was propagated at my school.

Unlike the YMCAs in some other parts of the world where the institution specifically caters to the working class, the Jerusalem Y established in 1931 was a centre of bustling social, intellectual, and athletic activities, and was housed in a monumental building that had a graceful high tower in the middle and was flanked by two domes, under one of which was a large auditorium with a stage, and under the other was the athletic department with a swimming pool in the basement; it had trees and a lovely garden in front and a large soccer pitch with rows of seats in the back. It was a landmark building of Jerusalem standing on Julian's Way opposite the majestic King David Hotel. Once inside it, one felt the plush atmosphere of the place with its modern furniture and shining cleanliness.

Its library had a large reading room with tables and chairs surrounded by comfortable leather armchairs; in this reading room were a card catalogue of the books, stands for the current newspapers and periodicals, and shelves with reference books and encyclopaedias. Its large collection of books was kept in an inner space behind the reception desk at which was a librarian always ready to fetch you the books whose catalogue numbers you gave him or her. This was a library different from the 'library' of the Christian Brothers' school and the crate collection of my father. Since Jerusalem had no public libraries, this was my first experience with a real library, and it was here that I continued to form myself intellectually. In it, I continued to regularly read *Al-Hilal* and *Al-Muqtataf* monthlies my father's collection had introduced me to, but also other literary journals like the then new Lebanese monthly *Al-Adib* of Albert Adib, the older Egyptian ones *Al-Risala* of Ahmad Hasan al-Zayyat and *Al-Thaqafa* of Ahmad Amin, as well as a newer one, *Al-Katib al-Misri* of Taha Hussein, and others. I also read more books by authors I had been introduced to through my father's collection, and discovered many, many more, including writers in English I began to admire, like Ernest Hemingway, John Steinbeck, Graham Greene, and Aldous Huxley. I also liked Marcel Proust, André Gide, and André Maurois. And it was at this Protestant institution's library that I first came to use *The Catholic Encyclopaedia* and *The Encyclopaedia of Islam*, whose existence I did not even know. In addition to all this, the courses I took with Jabra Ibrahim Jabra (1920-1994), who was my teacher of English literature at school and a member of the YMCA where he established the Jerusalem Arts Club after returning from Cambridge in 1943, gave me ideas what to read; the courses I took with Mounah Khouri (1918–1996), who taught me Arabic literature at school and was a member of the YMCA too (later Professor of Arabic Literature at Berkeley, California) gave me further ideas what to read. Both teachers became my friends and published writers, and I owe them much of my literary orientation.

Then I joined the University of London, where I earned a First Class BA (Honours) degree in Arabic and Islamic studies, and later a PhD in Arabic literature.

I did in fact become the teacher and educator first inspired by Khalil Sakakini, and for 56 years I taught, first in Palestine until 1968, then in USA (Hartford Seminary) until 1975, then in Canada (McGill University, Montreal) until my retirement in 2004. I was subsequently honoured by the Middle East Studies Association of North America (MESA) when its board bestowed upon me the 2004 Mentoring Award at the recommendation of my former students and my scholarly colleagues. Two of them (Kamal Abdel-Malek and Wael Hallaq) had edited a festschrift in my honour entitled *Tradition, Modernity, and Postmodernity in Arabic Literature: Essays in Honor of Professor Issa J. Boullata* (Brill, Leiden, 2000), to which twenty scholars among these former students and colleagues from the Middle East, Europe, USA, and Canada contributed literary articles. Moreover, I did become, like Khalil Sakakini, the author of many books.

I still do remember *The Little Red Hen* and Sitt Wasila's silent reading hour, and the romantic readings in my father's collection. Is it a wonder that my first book published in 1960 was on romanticism in modern Arabic poetry, and that my second one published in 1971 was on the Iraqi free verse poet, Badr Shakir al-Sayyab (its 6th edition has been published this July – Beirut, 2007).

Wordsworth's saying "The child is father of the man" cannot be truer than it is in my own life.

Acknowledgements

Grateful acknowledgement is made by the author and publisher to the following periodicals in which this book's short stories and essay first appeared:

"Without a Court Trial," *Banipal*, No. 5 (Summer 1999), pp. 77-78; "Bar-Room Confessions," *Banipal*, No. 8 (Summer 2000), pp. 60-62; "Third in Command," *Banipal*, Nos. 15/16 (Autumn 2002/Spring 2003), pp. 128-131; "Harvest of the Years," *Mizna*, Vol. 2, No. 2 (2000), pp. 15-17; "All is Vanity," *Banipal*, No. 12 (Autumn 2001), pp. 48-51; "Search for Saleema," *Banipal*, No. 6 (Autumn 1999), pp. 68-70; "A Retired Gentlemn," *Banipal*, No. 22 (Spring 2005), pp. 78-85; Books and I, *Banipal*, No. 29 (Summer 2007), pp. 34-42.

Other fiction titles from Banipal Books

*Order online from www.banipal.co.uk
or from your local bookshop*

Mordechai's Moustache and his Wife's Cats, and other stories by *Mahmoud Shukair, translated from Arabic*
ISBN 978-0-9549666-3-8   2007   pbk 124pp £7.99
First major publication in English from one of the most original of storytellers enthralls, surprises and even shocks. "Shukair's gift for absurdist satire is never more telling than in the hilarious title story"   **Judith Kazantzis**

The Myrtle Tree by *Jad el Hage*
ISBN 978-0-9549666-4-5 2007   pbk 288pp £9.99
"Better than any political analysis, this remarkable novel, set in a Lebanese mountain village, conveys with razor-sharp accuracy the sights, sounds, tastes and tragic dilemmas of Lebanon's fratricidal civil war."   **Patrick Seale**

Unbuttoning the Violin – *translated from Arabic and French*
ISBN 978-0-9549666-2-1   2006   pbk 128pp £3.95
Celebrating the UK tour, Banipal Live 2006, a paperback volume of selected works by poets Joumana Haddad from Lebanon and Abed Ismael from Syria, and fiction writers Mansoura Ez-Eldin from Egypt and Ala Hlehel from Palestine

An Iraqi in Paris by *Samuel Shimon, translated from Arabic*
ISBN 978-0-9549666-0-7 2005 pbk 252pp £11.99
Long-listed for the 2007 IMPAC Prize. "It's an Arabic answer to Miller's *Tropic of Cancer* – occasionally shocking; always witty and humane. Also included is his delightful memoir of an Iraqi childhood."   **Boyd Tonkin,** The Independent

Sardines and Oranges, short stories from North Africa by *21 Arab authors, translated from Arabic and French*
ISBN 978-0-9549666-1-4 2005   pbk 222pp £8.99
Tayeb Salih, Mohamed Choukri, Gamal el-Ghitani and Mohammed Dib are joined by other leading and newly emerging North African authors in this unique collaboration of the London Borough of Hammersmith and Fulham with Banipal Books

www.ingramcontent.com/pod-product-compliance
Lightning Source LLC
Chambersburg PA
CBHW020629250626
47154CB00004B/1734